W9-AAC-814

WHAT READERS ARE SAYING ABOUT THE HORSES OF HALF MOON RANCH:

"An exciting and page-turning book, perfect for horse lovers."

"A thrilling start to Horses of Half Moon Ranch. I would recommend anyone who is able to read it to do so."

"I couldn't put this book down!"

"An exciting and gripping read."

"This is the best book I have ever read. Jenny Oldfield's whole series is amazing...This story is so well described I would recommend it to all horse lovers."

"I totally love the Half Moon Ranch series by Jenny Oldfield. I've read nearly all of them and I can never put them down until I've finished them, they're so good."

"This story is one that I enjoyed. I hope that the author will continue to display such talent in writing."

"I found this book really thrilling and couldn't put it down."

"This is a good read for any horse lover. I enjoyed it a lot."

"You can fall in love with the adventurous story line, and get flown away to the Western U.S., where you will meet galloping horses under starlight. Gives the reader an interesting, always-on-the-move, adventurous, story line."

"I found this book very moving...I highly recommend [it]."

"Another great book by Jenny Oldfield."

"The best. I felt that I was there."

"Brilliant! I loved this book."

"I would recommend to any horse lover!"

THE HORSES OF
HALF MOON RANCH

THIRD-TIME
LUCKY

Jenny Oldfield

Published by Sourcebooks Jabberwocky, an imprint of Sourcebooks, Inc.
P.O. Box 4410, Naperville, Illinois 60567-4410
(630) 961-3900
Fax: (630) 961-2168
www.jabberwockykids.com

Originally published in Great Britain in 1999 by Hodder Children's Books.

Library of Congress Cataloging-in-Publication Data

Oldfield, Jenny.
  Third-time Lucky / Jenny Oldfield.
    p. cm. — (Horses of Half Moon Ranch ; bk. 6)
  Summary: When her beloved palomino horse, Lucky, contracts a mysterious and potentially fatal illness, thirteen-year-old Kirstie seeks out a legendary horse doctor who lives deep in the Rockies.
  [1. Horses—Fiction. 2. Ranch life—Colorado—Fiction. 3. Colorado—Fiction.] I. Title.
  PZ7.O4537Th 2009
  [Fic]—dc22
                              2008039734

Printed and bound in the United States of America.
VP 10 9 8 7 6 5 4 3 2

1

Kirstie Scott yawned as she crept out of her warm bed and struggled into cold jeans and sweatshirt.

She groaned as she fumbled her way downstairs, glancing at the clock in the hall. Two o'clock in the morning!

"Get a move on, Kirstie!" her brother, Matt, called from the porch. "You're the one who wanted to see this, remember!"

"Uh-uhh!" Eyes wouldn't stay open; fingers refused to work. "I've got a problem pulling my boots on!"

Matt grunted. "Follow me to the barn when you're ready, OK?"

Kirstie heard his footsteps cross the yard. Two o'clock! She should be fast asleep, not struggling with stupid boots. With three hard stamps she forced the second foot inside the tough leather casing, grabbed her cap from the hook by the door, and followed her brother outside.

Stars. A crescent moon. No clouds. Kirstie's slow brain registered the fine night. Pure habit took her from the ranch house across the yard to the open barn door. She yawned again, then shivered. It was cold at night, even in late April. Her breath came out as a small cloud of steam, and frost glinted on the cabin roofs up Apache Hill.

The barn was warm. Kirstie smelled the sweet scent of hay; cats were sleeping in dark corners. She stepped inside and pulled the door shut.

"Is that you, Kirstie?" Matt was already hard at work in the stall where the mare was due to foal. Overhead, there was a bare electric bulb. "Get rid of this soiled bedding, will you? And break open a new bale. We need extra straw in here."

She gave a final yawn, blinked, then shook herself fully awake as she rounded the corner. "Oh my!"

Taco, a black-and-white paint, was struggling to her feet. Then she raised her back feet to kick at her belly and tried to bite her swollen flanks. Through all this, Matt was attempting to wrap a bandage around her tail to keep it clean and neatly out of the way.

"She's already in labor," he gasped. "We've gotta move fast!"

Quickly Kirstie grabbed a rake and removed the soiled hay. She ran to break open a fresh bale and came back with armfuls to spread under Taco's feet. "What now?" she asked Matt, the expert.

He'd managed to fasten the bandage and now watched closely as the mare lay down and tried to roll. "We wait," he murmured.

"Can't we do something for her?" To Kirstie it looked like Taco was in a whole lot of pain.

"Nope." Firmly he backed Kirstie out of the stall. "Don't crowd her, OK? The foal's presenting normally, head first. Now it's up to Taco."

"Wow, how can you be so laid back?" Fully awake and alert to every movement of the mare, Kirstie began to pace up and down. The quiet barn echoed to the sound of her nervous footsteps. "I mean, I know you learn all this stuff at college, Matt, and it feels normal to you..." She turned and paced the length of the dark corridor between stalls. "...But I can't help getting uptight. Like, there's plenty that can go wrong, isn't there?" Another turn, more anxious striding past Matt, who stood quietly by Taco's stall. Kirstie didn't even dare to glance in at the pregnant mare. "Like, the foal could be in the wrong position and get stuck. Or it can't breathe after it's born. Or..." She clenched her hands until the fingernails dug into her palms.

"Kirstie!" her brother said calmly. He gestured for her to come back, then pointed to the deep straw bed where the mare lay.

"Oh ... wow!" A skinny, wet brown foal lay on its side beside Taco. "Oh ... ugh!" No way was this bit pretty, no matter how many times she saw it happen at Half Moon Ranch. The foal was surrounded by a slimy sack and attached to the mother by a bloody cord.

Matt smiled. "You want to dry him off?"

Gritting her teeth, Kirstie nodded. She edged

4

past her brother, picking up a handful of straw and approaching the newborn foal with great care.

Taco gave a low whinny to warn off the intruder, but as yet was too weak to stand.

Kirstie knew they were getting to the interesting bit now. Matt was about to try out a new technique that he'd learned at vet school called imprinting. But first, she knelt to rub the foal's coat. He raised his big, clumsy head to look at her, then flailed his feet in the straw. As she rubbed, the sticky, dark coat turned paler. It dried to a soft golden color, while his stumpy mane and tail were almost white.

"He's a palomino!" Kirstie whispered. Her favorite color of all, like her own horse, Lucky. Palominos shone in the sun like new gold. "Beautiful!"

Matt nodded and moved in. "Time to bond," he announced, telling Kirstie to hold Taco's head while he began to work with her foal. "'Give me a foal for his first hour on this earth, and he's mine for life!'"

"Who says?" Kirstie wasn't sure about this imprinting stuff, and neither was Taco. The mare wanted to be up on her feet, tending to her offspring herself.

"Brad Langer, my college principal. Say, Kirstie, you can let Taco lick and smell the foal while I work with him," he told her. "Yeah, head to head, that's great."

As the foal tried to rise, Matt held him down gently but firmly, all the while rubbing his head and neck. "This tells him, 'I'm the boss!' And he's taking it fine, see—he's letting himself relax."

"Easy, Taco!" Kirstie murmured. It was still hard for the mare to stand by and let this happen.

Slowly Matt moved his fingers over the foal's face and neck, then over his skinny withers and back. "The idea is, he gets used to the feel of my hands right from the word go," he explained. "That's the imprinting bit: learning to go with it now, while he's weak, instead of being able to fight it when he grows stronger."

"So he kind of thinks you're his parent."

Matt was gradually working his way around the foal's body, bending his legs, then stroking under his belly. "The way Mr. Langer tells it, this is how a foal learns respect for man from the moment he's born. A horse is a flight animal, but he's too young to flee. So I dominate him by holding him and stroking him all over, and he learns that's the way it's gonna be from now on."

"Hmm." Kirstie found herself frowning and having to hold hard to Taco's head collar. "I don't like the sound of that 'dominate.'"

"That's because you're too soft." Once Matt had stroked the foal from head to foot, he let him go. "Now we give him a chance to have his first feed. After a few hours, we come back and do it all over again."

Relieved, Kirstie let go of Taco's head and watched the mare and her newborn get into position to feed. "This feels better!" she sighed.

The foal sucked greedily, his sticklike legs splayed out, his head tilted back.

"Much too soft!" Matt laughed, though he too was satisfied to see the foal suckle strongly. "This imprinting stuff is supposed to work real well when we come to break a horse later on."

"'Break'!" Kirstie echoed, watching Matt reach for the light switch. There was another word she didn't like.

The light above the stall went off, and they felt their way out of the dark barn together. They crossed the yard by moonlight and kicked off their boots on the porch. Inside the house, a cozy bed waited and Kirstie realized she still felt dog-tired.

"You wanna come down and help with the imprinting stuff again?" Matt asked.

"When?" Did she, or didn't she? Kirstie wasn't sure.

"At dawn. We follow up a couple of hours after the first session." Matt took off his black Stetson, studying her doubtful frown. "What's getting to you, exactly?"

"I don't know. Something. Like, imprinting doesn't seem natural somehow." That was it; it meant coming between the mare and her newborn foal in an artificial way.

Matt nodded. "Not natural." He considered it. "But think about it, Kirstie. What's natural about putting a lead rein on a yearling? Is slinging a saddle on a colt's back what nature intended? Were we ever meant to climb on a horse's back and tighten a cinch under his belly?"

She sighed because she knew her tough-minded brother had a point. Left to nature, no horse would ever have been ridden. "No, but..."

8

Matt shook his head and took the stairs two at a time. "What's 'natural' got to do with it?" he insisted. "Ask yourself that next time you ride Lucky up Meltwater Trail!"

"He's right." Lisa Goodman took Matt Scott's side. "Honestly, Kirstie, Matt's doing a great job with little Moonshine. I really don't see your problem."

"Thanks, friend!" Kirstie urged Lucky into a trot, bushwhacking off Coyote Trail. She cut through a copse of slender aspen trees, heading up the steep hill toward an army of tall pines, seemingly marching shoulder to shoulder as far as Eagle's Peak. She'd hoped at least to have Lisa on her side.

"No, really!" Lisa followed on Snowflake, a five-year-old appaloosa which Kirstie's mom, Sandy Scott, had bought for Half Moon Ranch earlier that spring. The willing little brown and white mare soon caught up with Lucky. "Just because Matt's your big brother doesn't mean he's always wrong!"

"I never said he was always wrong!" Kirstie had wanted this to be a carefree ride, a rare chance to get away from the chores of the busy guest ranch.

She'd invited Lisa along, thinking they'd be on the same wavelength as usual. But when she'd started talking about the five-week-old foal, she'd opened up a big gap between them.

She'd said Matt had been going over-the-top these last few weeks with his imprinting theory. Moonshine wasn't being allowed to think for himself: all he'd learned to do was to submit. Lisa had said she thought it was kind of neat, the way the palomino foal followed Matt everywhere. He'd even had a head collar on him in the round pen, way before he was weaned, and anyone could go in and pick up his feet because he'd already learned to trust.

"You never said he was *always* wrong!" Lisa argued back. "But you don't have to—I can hear it in your voice!"

Kirstie clicked her tongue, the order for Lucky to lope. She felt him settle back onto his haunches then surge forward; she enjoyed the sensation of her long, fair hair blowing back from her face as the horse wove through the trees. But by the time they reached the ponderosa pines, Lucky was breathing hard, so she reined him back to a trot. Turning around in the saddle, she decided it was time to back down and enjoy the rest of the day. "OK, you win; my darling, handsome, hunky brother is right 100 percent of the time!"

Snowflake came to a sliding stop on the gravelly soil. Lisa pitched forward against her neck. When she righted herself, her thick, red, curly hair had tumbled over her eyes. "Hey, hold on! Did I say that?"

A broad grin lit up Kirstie's tanned face. "You don't have to!" she replied. "I can hear it in your voice!"

Lisa had denied everything: no way did she have a crush on Kirstie's big brother. Sure, he was tall and dark, but she wouldn't say handsome. Not even in spite of his hazel eyes. "He's twenty years old, for heaven's sakes!" she'd protested. "That's officially ancient!"

"I'll tell him that," Kirstie had threatened.

"You do and I'll never forgive you!" Lisa had pushed Snowflake on ahead, heading across country for a clearing in the trees.

Kirstie had watched the mare's smooth lope, her white tail streaming behind her, the pretty, white flecks on her coat picked out clearly in the shadows. Then she'd clicked her tongue and made a kissing sound. Lucky had taken off like a shot and thundered after Snowflake, his golden coat gleaming, his head loose and easy. By the time they'd reached Deer Lake, the two horses were neck and neck.

"Easy, Snowflake!" Lisa reined her horse back as soon as she spotted a couple of fishermen at the water's edge. The men wore rubber waders and stood thigh-deep in the crystal clear water, casting their lines far out into the lake with quiet concentration and skill.

"That's Dan Stewart." Kirstie recognized the red-checked shirt, bushy beard, and burly figure of one of that week's guests at Half Moon Ranch. He had three teenaged sons, Craig, Richie, and Brad, who had all headed out earlier that morning on an advanced ride with Hadley, the head wrangler. Dan, it seemed, had chosen the quieter pastime of fly-fishing.

"Hey, Kirstie!" The lawyer from New Hampshire greeted her as she and Lisa rode quietly by.

"Hey." She ducked her head shyly, letting her hair fall forward across her face.

"Did you see that little appie in the trees back there?" Dan inquired. With a quick flick of his wrist, he sent his line snaking through the air.

Kirstie shook her head, ready to ride on.

"A little appaloosa?" Lisa stopped. She was curious. "A Half Moon Ranch horse?"

"I guess not." Patiently, Dan Stewart cast out his line again. Sooner or later a fish would bite. "Looked like a kids' pony, not a ranch horse. I thought it was kinda strange: a pony all tacked up, running loose without a rider."

A few paces ahead of Lisa and Snowflake, Kirstie sat back in her saddle and reined Lucky in. A loose horse was something that needed to be sorted out. She turned Lucky and went to quiz Dan Stewart. "You're sure the rider wasn't around? Then how did the pony get to be here? Have you told anyone what you saw?"

Dan grunted and made her wait for answers. "You'd make a good prosecution lawyer, did anyone ever tell you?"

"Sorry," she blushed.

"No, that's OK. First, yes, I'm sure the pony was a runaway. I hollered for a rider to show up and didn't get any reply. Second, I have no idea how come she's running loose this far from civilization." He gazed around at the magnificent silent mountains rising above the snow line, their white peaks jutting into the blue sky. "And third, I'm telling you two what I saw right now!"

"Yeah, thanks!" Picking up that Kirstie was worried by the news, Lisa stepped in. "Where exactly did you see the pony?"

Dan didn't turn from his task, but nodded his head in the direction of the trees from which the girls had just emerged. "Back there, five minutes ago."

"C'mon." Letting Lisa thank the fisherman, Kirstie retraced her steps. She noticed Lucky prick his ears and point them forward, listening intently. His keen hearing had already picked up something unusual. Then, as he re-entered the forest, he curled his lip, threw back his head and gave a high, loud whinny.

"Good boy!" Kirstie leaned forward to pat his neck. Peering between the tall, scaly trunks of the pine trees, she saw a tiny chipmunk scoot across the trail, his boldly striped tail sailing behind like a black-and-white banner.

"Anything?" Lisa came up quietly beside her.

"Nope. Lucky heard something, but he didn't get an answer." Softly, Kirstie urged him forward. She watched the moving shadows where sunlight filtered through the trees, listened, and let her horse take the lead.

Deeper into the wood—rich with the smell of pine resin—over fallen trunks, pushing aside brushwood, Kirstie and Lucky went searching for the runaway pony. A glance over her shoulder told her that Lisa had decided to wait with Snowflake on the trail in case there was anything to be seen back there.

Lucky went on, his feet falling softly on the cushion of pine needles. The shadows closed in as the trees grew thicker. Soon, Lisa and Snowflake were out of sight.

"Easy!" Kirstie murmured. She trusted Lucky's judgment on this. His ears were still up, his whole body alert. He stopped, turned his head to listen, changed direction, and walked steadily on.

He stopped when they came to a large, smooth rock shaped like a dome. It had brilliant pink paintbrush flowers growing at its base and the trunk of a half-felled tree resting against one side. Kirstie noticed with a faint shiver the exposed roots reaching out of the earth like gnarled witches' fingers. "Here?" she whispered to Lucky.

The palomino stood full square, his head turned to the ten-foot-high rock.

Quietly Kirstie dismounted. She needed to find a way around the back of the rock without breaking her neck on the loose shale slope. Maybe climbing up it would be better. Footholds were hard to find in the pink granite, but she managed it and eased herself up to the top of the dome.

Lying flat on her stomach, peering down the far side, Kirstie saw the pony.

The tiny spotted horse had got her wide saddle and bulky stirrups wedged between a tree and the rock. She was six feet away, looking up at Kirstie with wild eyes and flaring nostrils. Her hooves scraped and pawed at the rocky ground, but the more she struggled, the tighter she wedged herself.

In spite of the little pony's distress, Kirstie saw

right away what she had to do to help. Once she got down there and unbuckled the cinch strap, she could ease the saddle off and set the poor creature free.

"OK, hang on in there," she whispered, scrambling over the top of the rock. "I'll have you out in a couple of minutes, no problem."

2

"The strange thing is, you'd expect her to have worked up a sweat, but she feels real cold." Kirstie ran her hand down the appaloosa's neck. A nimble scramble down the rock, making sure to keep out of the way of the small but still lethal hooves, had brought her alongside the trapped pony. She'd moved in close, saying soothing words all the while, until the poor thing had calmed down enough to stay quiet as Kirstie unbuckled the cinch. As predicted, once the saddle was loose and she was able to lift it, the pony quickly squirmed free.

Lisa and Snowflake had decided to follow Kirstie and Lucky after all, and it was at the moment when the pony broke loose that they drew level with the dome-shaped rock. They'd blocked the pony's escape route as, relieved of her saddle, she'd blundered through the undergrowth and shot out across the track. She'd reared and turned, but had been stopped again by Lucky standing in the way. Meanwhile, Kirstie struggled after her, carrying the battered saddle.

Really it had been no contest: Lisa and Snowflake, Kirstie and Lucky against an eleven-hands-high pony. Lisa had unhitched a rope from her saddle horn and handed it to Kirstie, who had quickly looped it around the runaway's neck.

And now that Kirstie was running a hand down the little appie's side, she was puzzled. The pony must have been jammed between the tree and the rock for at least five minutes, working hard to break free. Yet she definitely felt cold and clammy.

"It must be the trauma of being trapped," Lisa suggested, then went to search in Snowflake's saddlebag. "What have we got to help keep her warm?" She drew out her waterproof slicker that she wore only when it rained. "Any good?"

"No thanks." Kirstie thought that the best thing to do was to get the shocked horse moving. "Let's lead her back to the ranch, then call around to see if any kid has taken a fall and gone home without her pony."

"Can she walk OK?" Lisa pointed to the cuts on her knees and fetlocks, where she'd bashed herself against the rock.

Kirstie lifted the pony's dainty feet to check, feeling her sides heave rapidly in and out. Her breath seemed to rasp inside her chest, probably another sign that she was in shock. But as far as the legs went, there seemed to be no reason why she couldn't make it safely to Half Moon Ranch.

"She doesn't care about you messing with her," Lisa commented, noting how the pretty pony turned her head to follow Kirstie's every move. The horse let her attach a lead rope securely to the head collar that she wore under her bridle and was then ready to follow.

"She's great!" Smiling, Kirstie gave her nose a rub, appreciating the dished shape which gave her the look of a high-class Arabian. The pony's eyes were large, her ears pointed, dainty again. Yet her withers were strong for a horse of her size, and when she walked forward, her stride was long and straight.

"Yeah, well, don't get too attached." Lisa smiled as Kirstie remounted. They were ready to leave: Lisa with the pony's saddle slung across Snowflake's broad hindquarters, Kirstie and Lucky leading the runaway. "There's an owner out there somewhere!" Lisa reminded her. "This pretty little lady has a home to go to, so don't start making any plans!"

"Neat work, honey!" Sandy Scott congratulated Kirstie as she took the appaloosa pony into the barn and found an empty stall in which to bed her down. "Someone's gonna be real happy you and Lisa took the trouble to bring her in."

Kirstie's mom had got back from leading the intermediate riders and heard the tale from Lisa. She'd just found time before the evening barrel race to come out and check the situation in the barn.

"She's pretty, isn't she?" Kirstie spread an extra layer of hay to make sure the visitor was comfortable.

"Yep. Pony of the Americas," Sandy noted.

"Eye-catching, that's for sure. The breed began in Mason City, Iowa, back in the '50s; a cross between a Shetland pony and an appaloosa mare. Now they're everywhere."

"Should I put a blanket on her?" Kirstie asked, her voice edged with concern. "She's still cold."

"OK." Sandy leaned next door to unhitch a spare hay net from little Moonshine's stall. The palomino foal nickered and came to poke her head around the corner. "Give the appie this to eat and plenty of fresh water. Then come on out to the corral. Barrel racing's about ready to start."

So Kirstie worked fast to follow her mom, making a fuss of the appaloosa and giving her everything she might need to get over her ordeal by Deer Lake. When she emerged into the daylight, the first person she met up with in the sunny yard was Tommy Woodford, the San Luis vet's fifteen-year-old son. The second person was Lisa.

"Would you believe it!" Lisa cried, running over from the ranch house with a broad smile. "Word travels fast. We already found the appie's owners!"

"What appie?" Tommy wanted to know. Like his dad, he was dark haired and tanned. He wore a white T-shirt, jeans, a brown Stetson, and boots, ready to take part in the barrel racing contest. "What owners?"

"Hold on a minute, Tommy!" Kirstie cut in. "What do you mean, you found them?"

"I called my grandpa over at Lone Elm to tell him what happened. He called Smiley Gilpin at the Forest Guard station. Smiley had heard about some nine-year-old kid who fell off her pony yesterday afternoon near Red Eagle Lodge."

"But that's by Bear Hunt Overlook," Kirstie pointed out as the three of them walked toward the corral. A crowd of about thirty people had gathered at the fence, ready for the evening's events. "Miles away from here."

"Yeah, but Grandpa called the family. Their name's Gostin and they're here on vacation. They have a lodge house along Timberline Trail. And the pony's a white and black appie called Whisper." Lisa checked the facts off on her fingers. "She's been loose almost twenty-four hours, easily enough time for her to make her way over to Deer Lake."

"OK." With a sigh Kirstie was forced to give in

to the evidence. She grabbed the top rung of the fence and slung her leg over, settling in to watch the race. "It's their pony for sure."

"Tough." Lisa climbed up beside her and gave her a small, sympathetic grin. "But, hey, think of how great the Gostin kid's gonna feel when she hears the news!"

"The aim is to get around those barrels in the fastest time possible." Tommy Woodford explained the rules to Richie Stewart. "You just give your horse his head and let the sucker blast out of the starting gate and around the course. You rein him around the barrels as best you can. If you're still in the saddle when you hit the exit, you've got a chance."

"Go for it!" Lisa urged. "Kirstie and me are entered."

"Yeah, but..." The visitor from New Hampshire frowned uncertainly. His older brother, Craig, had just fallen off his horse and landed in the dust. Next it was his younger brother Brad's turn on Crazy Horse.

"What have you got to lose?" Lisa asked.

"My pride!" came the swift reply from the fair-haired boy. "I'd hardly even been on a horse before I came to Half Moon Ranch."

"So?"

"So I don't have a chance of winning against you guys." Richie looked on nervously as a ten-year-old dude rider shot out of the starting gate on Jitterbug. The sorrel mare raced for the nearest barrel, made a sliding stop in a cloud of yellow dust and turned. Then she loped hard for the next barrel.

"If that kid can do it, so can you." Taking no argument from Richie, Lisa dragged him down from the fence and across to Charlie, whose job it was to enter the competitors on a list. "Richie Stewart," she told the junior wrangler. "Put him on Rodeo Rocky, OK!"

Back on the fence, Kirstie grinned at Tommy. "Lisa likes him," she explained wryly. "That's just her way of showing it."

"He's not happy." Tommy grinned back, jumping to the ground and pulling on a pair of leather gloves. It was his turn to ride. The kid on Jitterbug had achieved a time of fifty-two seconds, the fastest so far.

"Who are you riding?" Kirstie asked, going along to the starting point with Tommy in order to get Lucky ready.

"Johnny Mohawk."

She wished him luck on the high-spirited black gelding, slipped into the barn for a quick look at the little appie, then back into the corral in time to see the vet's son complete the course in forty-nine seconds flat. The crowd applauded as Tommy slid from the saddle. Then they fell quiet again as a tense-looking Richie Stewart came up to the starting gate. Kirstie saw Matt open the gate and Rocky blast out into the arena. The bay's coat gleamed in the sun; his black mane and tail streamed out as he made the first barrel in record time, spun on a spot the size of a silver dollar, then raced on.

Kirstie grinned. Rodeo Rocky was in his element, despite his relatively novice rider. He showed off his amazing bursts of speed in front of an audience. His wild past on the plains of Wyoming showed through in the smoothness of his action, the power of his bunched muscles. And, to his credit, Richie hung on through all the twists and turns, giving the horse his head and coming out with a time of forty-seven seconds.

"C'mon, Lucky, that's our target." Kirstie led her palomino to line up behind Lisa and Snowflake.

Lucky held back until the gate was clear, making room for Richie and Rodeo Rocky to pass by. The boy from New Hampshire was breathless and triumphant, but trying not to show it. "Cool!" he told Kirstie, sliding from the saddle and leading his horse away.

Out in the arena, Lisa was not so lucky. She and Snowflake made the third of the six barrels in good time, but then they misjudged the turn. Snowflake swerved wide and fast, running Lisa up against the fence.

"Ooh!" The crowd gasped and jumped back in the nick of time. Snowflake thundered by, Lisa's left stirrup hit the fence, and her foot slipped out. "Aah!" Another cry as the horse slid to an uncontrolled halt and tipped her unbalanced rider forward over the saddle horn.

"Wow!" Richie Stewart looked back in time to see Lisa part company with Snowflake. She tumbled headfirst over the horse's neck, did a complete forward flip, and landed on her butt.

"Unintentional dismount," Kirstie murmured. She could tell right away that the only thing her friend had injured was her pride. As Lisa grabbed her baseball cap from the dust and went to take hold of Snowflake's reins, Kirstie stuck her foot in Lucky's stirrup and swung up into the saddle.

"Forty-seven to beat!" she murmured in her horse's ear. "We can do it!"

Matt swung open the gate, and they took off at a full gallop. Responding to the crowd's cheers, the palomino gave it everything he had.

"...Eight point five seconds!" Charlie announced as Kirstie and Lucky rounded the first barrel.

She reined him to the left, tilting her shoulders, going with the smooth movement of the horse. Lucky shook his head, made a tight turn, and trucked on.

"...Twenty-three seconds!" Charlie gave Kirstie's time at the halfway point. Dust rose from the arena into the golden evening light. Shadows fell long and cool across the open space.

"C'mon, Lucky!" she urged. She felt a split

second's hesitation, a momentary loss of will. But the palomino gathered himself and went on.

"Thirty-six seconds!" Charlie yelled.

Two barrels to go. Kirstie saw the sweat on Lucky's neck, heard him suck in breath for the final effort.

"You can do it!" Lisa cried. "Go, go, go!"

"...Forty-eight point five seconds!" Charlie gave the final time as Kirstie and Lucky raced through the finishing gate.

"Tough." Lisa came up to them to commiserate. "One and a half seconds outside Richie's time."

Kirstie nodded and dismounted. With only one more competitor to go, it looked like the visitor had won.

"I guess you couldn't concentrate," Lisa said quietly as Kirstie led Lucky away. Both girls knew that Kirstie could usually make a better time. "Your mind must have been on little Whisper."

"Not really," Kirstie had to admit. She tethered Lucky to a post and quickly untacked him. "I was trying real hard. It was Lucky whose mind wasn't on the job."

Seeming to pick up her disappointment, he dropped his head and gave a short cough.

She wrapped an arm around his neck and rested against him. Poor Lucky, he knew he could have won the race and didn't enjoy letting Kirstie down. Now he looked sad and down.

It made her feel bad, too. So she stroked him and whispered sweet nothings in his ear, to let him know the barrel race didn't matter. What mattered was him and her. Nothing else.

Lucky nuzzled Kirstie's cheek with his soft white nose. *Sorry*, he said in his gentle, wordless way.

"No problem," she murmured. "You helped rescue the little appie, didn't you? That's enough for one day!"

"We had to get over to Half Moon Ranch fast, because we leave Colorado tomorrow," Pamela Gostin told Sandy Scott. She did all her daughter's talking for her.

The Gostins' trailer stood in the yard, gleaming in the moonlight. It was nine thirty, and the excitement of the barrel race had long since died down. Richie Stewart had accepted his winner's plaque to general applause, and Lisa had taken him and his brothers off to celebrate in town. Shortly afterward,

Whisper's owners had showed up to reclaim their runaway pony.

Kirstie led the small group into the barn, listening to Pamela Gostin's explanation.

"The pony's a little hard for Lacey to handle sometimes. She spooks easy at any small thing, not like these steady old trail horses you have at the ranch."

Less of the old, Kirstie thought, *and less of the steady*. The horses of Half Moon Ranch had as much spirit as any she knew. She led the Gostin kid and her mom along the row of stalls, past Moonshine and Taco who were stabled together for the night.

"So what spooked Whisper yesterday?" Sandy asked the girl kindly.

"It was kind of weird," Pamela Gostin cut in. She was a small, overweight woman dressed in a bright red suede leather jacket, with her long, glossy dark hair pinned back Spanish style. "Lacey's big brother, Wade, was riding with her. He says Whisper just bucked without warning. Before they knew it, she'd dumped Lacey and galloped off. Their father didn't take the news too well, I can tell you. Why,

32

the tack alone on that pony's back is worth over two thousand dollars!"

Kirstie's mom's smile faded. So far, neither Lacey nor her mother had even thanked them or asked how the pony was. "So anyway, it turned out OK in the end," she said pointedly.

By this time, Kirstie was busy in Whisper's stall. "Did you bring trailer bandages?" she asked the Gostins. "Your pony cut her legs when she got trapped. They need some protection while you drive her home."

Frowning, Pamela Gostin shook her head. "Maybe we can borrow some from you?"

Nodding her reply, Sandy helped Kirstie by gathering up the pony's saddle and bridle. "Here." She handed the silent daughter the bridle to carry. "Kirstie will lead Whisper out and load her into the trailer for you."

The sooner, the better, Kirstie said to herself. *Poor pony. With owners like this, I'd pretty soon run away myself!* They showed no relief, no gratitude, nothing. In fact, she suspected they didn't even like their sweet little horse.

She was glad when they had Whisper out of the

barn and into the waiting trailer. People like the Gostins made her sad and angry.

"Bye." Sandy shook hands with the mother as Kirstie bolted the trailer shut. Inside the box, Whisper stood tethered and shivering.

"Thanks for your help," Pamela Gostin said, cool and formal. "Finding the pony means we can set off for home early tomorrow morning, as planned." She gave the briefest of smiles, then ordered her daughter into the cab.

Kirstie took one last look at the miserable appaloosa pony. "Bye, Whisper," she murmured. She went to stand by her mom while the trailer drove slowly out of the yard, its red tail lights glowing in the dark.

There was a deep frown on Sandy's face as she stood, arms crossed, watching the Gostins leave. Then, "C'mon!" she said briskly to Kirstie. "Don't say a word, OK! Forget about them. Time for hot chocolate and bed!"

3

"How's your new method with Taco's foal coming along?" Hadley asked Matt over breakfast the next morning. Though it was changeover day at the ranch, when old guests left and new ones came in, there was still a long list of chores to get through. The old ranch hand grabbed a chance to talk between mouthfuls of coffee, before he and Charlie started to bring the horses in from the remuda to pick out their hooves, ready for the shoer, Chuck Perry.

Matt swallowed the last of his eggs and bacon before putting his hat on. "Moonshine? We're doing great. That's where I'm going right now. Come and take a look if you've got the time." With a grin in his kid sister's direction, he quickly left the kitchen.

"Kirstie doesn't approve," Sandy explained. "She thinks imprinting is tough on both the foal and the mare."

"Uh-huh." Hadley picked up his own battered white hat from the table.

Spotting a possible ally, Kirstie rushed in with her point of view. "This imprinting stuff looks over-the-top to me. For instance, you have to press down on the foal's back as soon as it can stand. It's supposed to get it ready to accept a saddle later in life. But I reckon a day-old foal deserves to be left in peace!"

"So you've been giving Matt a hard time?" Hadley strode out onto the porch to look for Charlie.

"Me?" She jumped the step into the yard, turned and spread her arms wide. How could the old man possibly think that?

"Yeah, you." Hadley gave her to understand she should lay off Matt. "Your brother don't act cruel to horses as a general rule, does he? So I'd say give the boy a chance to try what he learned in school."

"How about you, Charlie?" Kirstie turned to him for help as he emerged from the bunkhouse.

"Come again?" Hadley's junior ran the tap outside the door and splashed his face with cold water.

"Charlie's got work to do!" Hadley insisted, dragging him off to Red Fox Meadow without so much as a cup of coffee to start the day.

Defeated, Kirstie kicked a stone across the yard and headed for the barn. She remembered she'd left Lucky's tack in there after yesterday's barrel race, instead of hanging it up in the tack room as usual. And while she was there, she thought she might as well take a look at Matt and Moonshine, not that she would ever agree with imprinting, habituation, desensitizing and all that fancy vet school stuff.

She swung through the door into the barn and walked along the row of stalls until she came to Moonshine's. But instead of finding her brother hard at work training the tiny palomino foal to get used to ropes and the feel of his hands, she saw him standing a few feet away from Moonshine, studying him with a puzzled frown.

"Hey, Kirstie." Hands in pockets, he glanced up.

"Something wrong?" She, too, looked hard at

the foal. His head was down and he blinked back at her with dull, lifeless eyes.

"He didn't eat his hay." Matt jerked his thumb at the manger. "And you see the patches of sweat on his neck?"

She nodded. "Could be a fever. Did you take his temperature?"

"Yeah. It's way up past a hundred and three."

"So what is it?" Easing her way into the stall, she realized that the foal was trembling all over and unsteady on his feet. She felt a small knot twist up in her stomach as she waited for Matt's verdict.

"Could be something he ate," he suggested. "Or worms in his gut."

"You don't sound like you think it's that." Kirstie could tell that Matt was turning things over in his mind. "What about colic?"

He shook his head. "Nope. He's not going down and trying to roll, see."

"What then?" The knot in Kirstie's stomach was tightening. She wanted to go forward and reassure Moonshine, but something held her back. Instead, she looked hard into Matt's eyes for an answer.

A deep frown guarded his own feelings. He swallowed hard and spoke in a strained voice. "Equine influenza."

Horse flu. "You sure?"

"No. We need Glen Woodford to take a look." Matt sighed and started to walk away. "Pray that I'm wrong," he told Kirstie. "But just in case I'm right, you'd best clear all the other foals and mares out of here fast as you can!"

"How can it be horse flu?" Sandy Scott demanded. "Our vaccination schedule is up to date. TT, rhino, tetanus, influenza—Glen and Tommy came over and gave them their shots early last month."

Kirstie knew that her mom took pride in the ranch's health program. The idea that an outbreak of influenza was possible at Half Moon Ranch seemed not to have sunk in yet. But Kirstie had immediately done what Matt had told her and taken the young horses out of the barn into the corral and started to heap the soiled bedding onto a cart. They would have to carry the straw outside and burn it to destroy any bugs it might contain.

"Think about it," Sandy insisted, waiting anxiously

for the vet to arrive. She paced up and down the barn, glancing in every now and then at the sick foal. "Taco had her jabs along with the rest. If the mare was vaccinated one month prior to foaling, Moonshine should have passive transfer through the colostrum."

"That could be the problem here," Matt admitted. He spoke slowly, as if reluctant to go on.

Kirstie put down her rake and went closer. She knew that colostrum was the name given to the first feed the foal would take from the mother's udder. It contained important protection against disease.

"You know I was working with Moonshine from the start?" Matt reminded Sandy. "Well, I guess that could've gotten in the way of his first feed. He took the udder after I'd finished my first session, but I really can't be sure that he took what he needed."

Sandy took a deep breath. "How do you mean?"

"He didn't feed for long, just didn't seem interested. And Taco didn't stick around. To tell you the truth, Mom, the mare hasn't been a good mother. I've had to give the foal extra milk and now solids to keep up his weight."

"You're saying they didn't bond?" Sandy took it in gradually. "And that could be to do with your imprinting method? Oh, Matt, why didn't you tell me?"

Kirstie bit her lip to stop herself from exploding. *See!* she wanted to yell. *What did I tell you?* Instead, she walked quickly away from Matt and Sandy into the open. "And now Moonshine's sick because of Matt and his stupid theory!" she muttered out loud when she was sure there was no one to hear.

But that still didn't explain everything. She understood now that Moonshine might not have the resistance all young foals needed against disease. But if it was horse flu and Glen confirmed it, where had the virus come from in the first place?

Like her mom said, all Half Moon Ranch horses were up to date with their health program.

Kirstie didn't have time to work out the solution to the mystery, as she spotted Glen Woodford's black jeep speeding down the hill toward the ranch. She ran across the yard to greet him and Tommy, almost falling over herself to tell them what had happened. "Matt says it could be equine flu!" she gasped.

The vet listened and nodded, grabbing his bag from the back of the jeep and striding toward the barn. "You'd better hope he's wrong," he muttered.

"How bad does this flu get?" she wanted to know, ignoring Tommy and running alongside Glen.

"Pretty bad." He paused at the door and gave it to her straight. "Equine influenza in an adult horse can cause long term damage to the internal organs and the nervous system."

Kirstie's eyes widened. Damage to stuff like the heart and lungs, the whole of a horse's nerve network and senses! The answer could hardly have been worse, but there was more to come. "And?"

"And equine influenza in a foal under three months can be fatal," he told her quietly, taking her arm and leading her out of the sun into the dark barn. "So, c'mon, honey, let's get in there fast and see if we can save little Moonshine for you."

"You keep him warm; you bandage his legs," the vet instructed. "'He needs a good bed of fresh straw, no drafts getting in during the night."

Sandy Scott listened quietly, head down. She

wasn't looking at Matt, who stood behind Glen, his face blank with misery. The diagnosis of equine influenza had just been confirmed.

"If he'll take milk from a bottle, give it little and often, OK?" The vet waited for Sandy to confirm that she was taking this in. "I'm gonna give you an electuary—a thick paste—for his cough. Matt, you can smooth it onto the back of his tongue with a spatula."

"You hear that?" Kirstie was kneeling in the straw beside the sick foal. "We're gonna make you better."

Moonshine lay on his side, his legs folded, his head against the straw. Making an effort to raise his head, he licked her hand, then sank back.

In spite of her promise, Kirstie knew that the foal was going downhill fast. "Can't you give him a shot of something?" she pleaded with Glen.

He took a deep breath and shook his head. "This is a virus. Antibiotics won't work. And it's highly infectious, so no other horse must come near, OK?"

"What about the ones that have been in contact lately?" Kirstie thought back over twenty-four hours, her mind still reeling from the diagnosis and what it might mean. She kept one hand on Moonshine's neck, feeling the cold clamminess of his soft golden coat.

"Taco?" Glen asked.

"Yes, and the other foals."

The vet turned to Tommy and asked him to run to the jeep and bring back the file where he kept records of the vaccination programs for all the ranches he looked after. When his son returned, Glen asked him to check the list.

"Fine," Tommy told Sandy. "Taco had her shots last month, so no problem there. All the foals over three months had their shots, too."

Kirstie's mom gave a short sigh of relief. "We'll keep Moonshine in quarantine in any case," she decided. "Best not to take a risk of spreading the darned thing."

Still Matt hung back. Looking at his strained, tense face, even Kirstie began to feel sorry for him.

"So how come the foal fell sick?" Glen went on to ask, packing his bag. His broad back bent over the foal for one final look seemed to Kirstie to offer a scrap of reassurance. "You don't have any new arrivals on the ranch that haven't been Coggins tested?"

"No way!" Sandy replied quickly. "The last horse we bought was Snowflake, way back in early spring. And we ran all the tests before we let her loose with the remuda."

"No new arrivals," Glen echoed with a shake of his head. "I don't get it."

"Unless..." Matt spoke for the first time in ages. He flashed Kirstie then Sandy a quick look of alarm.

A new arrival...a horse that hadn't been vaccinated, coming into contact not necessarily with the main herd in Red Fox Meadow, but with the foals in the barn.

...A horse from who knew where, whose owners might not have kept up with the booster shots.

...The sort of owners who didn't know much about health programs and cared even less about their pony.

...The Gostins, for instance.

"Whisper!" Kirstie breathed the name, remembering the strange coldness of her spotted coat, the trembling of her limbs. Not shock, after all. Not the trauma of being trapped between the rock and the tree, but equine influenza.

Of course, it was the runaway appaloosa who had brought the killer virus to Half Moon Ranch!

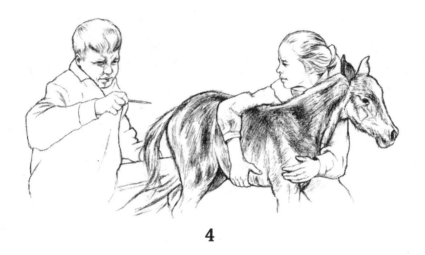

4

"You count yourselves lucky that you only have the little palomino foal who's at risk of catching the disease," Glen Woodford told Sandy, Matt and Kirstie as they stood together in the yard. "I've seen equine influenza spread like wildfire through herds where the owners don't have their program of inoculations up to date."

"I don't feel lucky," Kirstie told Tommy. She helped him load his dad's kit into the back of the jeep. "What I feel is dumb. Like, I was the idiot who brought a seriously sick pony to Half Moon Ranch!"

"So how were you to know?" The boy mumbled a reassurance. He was a serious, shy kid who didn't push himself forward, but who was often around to help his dad do the straightforward ranch work.

"I wasn't. But I was dumb not to figure out that Whisper was sick. And maybe deep down I did know. She was in bad trouble when I brought her in, but I was stupid and put it down to shock. I didn't give it enough thought." Miserably determined to blame herself, Kirstie's mind went over and over the events of the previous day.

"You're not the vet around here," Tommy reminded her. "How come Matt or Sandy didn't think of it either?"

"Too busy, I guess." Kirstie stood back as Tommy slammed the door of the jeep. "What I'm really saying is, none of this would've happened if I hadn't stormed in and rescued the pony. That's me; I don't stop to think!"

"Hey, honey!" Sandy had overheard and came to put an arm around Kirstie's shoulder. "No one's to blame here, you understand? Matt did what he's been taught at school without seeing the downside. You did a good deed and that hasn't worked

48

out either. Now we all need to work together to help Moonshine pull through."

Kirstie nodded. "What about Whisper? Who's gonna take care of her?"

"The Gostins," Sandy said firmly. "I'll call Smiley and ask him to drive up Timberline Trail to their lodge. If they haven't left for home already, he can warn them that they have a real sick pony on their hands."

"And if he's too late?" she wanted to know. She pictured the uncaring family driving their trailer halfway across America without even realizing that Whisper needed medical care.

Sandy sighed and shrugged. "Not our problem," she murmured. "Tough, but that's life."

Later that day, Lisa came to help Kirstie and Matt nurse the sick foal. She'd been planning to spend the day with her grandfather, Lennie Goodman, at Lone Elm Trailer Park, until the two of them had received a visit from the Forest Guard and Smiley Gilpin had told them the latest news: two cases of equine influenza in the neighborhood, one at Half Moon Ranch. Lisa had persuaded her grandpa to drive her over there as fast as he could.

She arrived at midday, dressed in a blue T-shirt and denim shorts, her face hot and sticky from the drive.

"Did Smiley get to the Gostins in time?" Kirstie asked. She knelt in the straw holding Moonshine steady while Matt took his temperature.

"No way. Their house was shuttered and locked. A guy who lives up the trail said he thought they were from Texas. He heard them set off at dawn."

"Texas is a big state," Matt said, shaking his head as he read the thermometer. "Still way too high," he commented.

Kirstie stroked the foal, then began to wipe his face with a clean, cool cloth. "He's not taking milk," she told Lisa, "which means he's losing fluids fast. And Matt just took his pulse."

"How was that?" Lisa looked from one to the other, obviously upset by the foal's condition. She crouched beside Kirstie, her eyes moist and glistening in the gloom of the darkened stall.

"Fast and weak," Matt reported. "His breathing's not too good either."

Lisa put a hand on Moonshine's frail ribcage to

feel the uneven movement as his lungs struggled for breath.

"It's the respiratory problem that we have to watch," Matt warned. "I can replace the fluids through a drip, but if the little guy can't get enough oxygen, we're in real trouble."

"C'mon!" Kirstie leaned over the foal to whisper encouragement. She let her fair hair fall forward to mask the tears that had sprung to her eyes. "Don't give up."

Without taking her gaze off the patient, Lisa sat back on her heels. "How long since you took a break?" she asked Kirstie.

"I don't know. A few hours." In truth, she hadn't left off nursing Moonshine since Glen and Tommy Woodford had driven away. Since then she'd watched every tremble of the foal's weak limbs, heard the catch in every congested breath. "Why?"

"Why not let Matt take over?" Lisa suggested. "Come into the house and have a cool drink."

"I can't." A dread came over Kirstie at the mere thought of stepping away from Moonshine's side.

"Yes, you can," Lisa insisted. "Matt will be here, won't you?"

He nodded without speaking, unable to meet Kirstie's gaze as she looked up at him with tearful eyes.

"Moonshine knows Matt better than anyone," Lisa said, more gently than before. "He'll be OK if Matt stays with him."

It was true. Kirstie had a sudden picture of the healthy little palomino trotting after her brother across the corral, shadowing his every step. His coat had shone gold in the sun. Matt had stopped and turned to stroke him, had called him a cute little guy, had grinned at the prancing, dancing steps the foal had taken. "Scoot!" he'd laughed, shooing him off, laughing again when Moonshine had ignored him and kept on trying to follow him into the tack room.

That had been Friday, before this whole nightmare had begun.

Slowly, letting her hand linger for a few more seconds on the foal's neck, Kirstie stood up. "I'm going with Lisa," she told her brother. "We'll be at the house if you need us."

"Grandpa says he's real sorry about Moonshine,"

Lisa told Kirstie. She sat with her in the shade of the porch swing, sipping orange juice, looking out at the snowy summit of Eagle's Peak in the far distance.

Lost in a long series of regrets that came out as sighs, Kirstie didn't respond. If only they hadn't ridden Lucky and Snowflake up to Deer Lake. If only Dan Stewart had continued fishing instead of stopping to tell them about the runaway horse … Her gaze drifted down from the mountaintops, across the dark-forested slopes, along the green ribbon of flat pasture land in the valley bottom to the red roofs of the ranch buildings. Finally, she fixed her attention on two tiny brown hummingbirds who came to sip sugar water from the clear plastic dish hanging in the porch.

Lisa talked on to fill the silence. "According to Grandpa, horse flu has been bad news as far back as he can recall. Way back, before they invented a vaccine, a horse would get real sick with it. You got so much as a cough out of one of the cutters or reiners used by the old cowboys and, boy, that horse was off the ranch quicker than you could blink."

Kirstie closed her eyes and sighed. *Don't give up, Moonshine!*

"Once a horse caught flu, he was no earthly use. A cowboy needs a strong, healthy horse he can rely on, not one with a breathing problem or a weak heart. And Grandpa said quarter horses didn't cost a whole lot when he was young. A cowboy needed a good, well made saddle, but a horse could be bought and sold real cheap."

"What's money got to do with it?" Kirstie murmured. *Fight this, Moonshine! Prove them wrong!*

"Oh sure, I agree. And sometimes, even in those days, a cowboy would love his horse. I mean, really love him!" Lisa hurried on. "I remember Grandpa told me once about a guy he knew here at Half Moon when your grandpa ran it as a cattle ranch. The guy's name was Red Mitchell and he owned a black-and-white paint named Bandit. Red worked Bandit on roundups, spring and fall, for ten years or more. Then the horse got sick."

Gradually Kirstie tuned in to Lisa's story. Mention of her grandfather, Chuck Glassner, made her recall the endless summer days when, as little kids, she and Matt had visited Half Moon Ranch. They would leave the choked, dusty streets of Denver where they used to live and drive out here for the summer with their mom and dad. That was before their dad had left them to start a new family with another woman, before their mom had sold the Denver house and moved them out to the ranch for good. "What did this Red Mitchell do about his sick horse?" she murmured, her gaze fixed on the darting, hovering hummingbirds.

"He took Bandit west, deep into the Rockies, to see some special horse doctor. Red was part Native American. The horse doctor he knew out there had connections with an ancient tribe. He used cures dreamed up by the old medicine men, herbs and stuff." Lisa hesitated as she saw Matt's tall figure appear in the barn doorway and she felt Kirstie suddenly sit forward. But she went on trying to distract her friend as he walked slowly toward them.

"The point is, Red Mitchell cared enough about his old ranch horse to take two weeks out of work to drive Bandit hundreds of miles looking for a cure..."

Kirstie stood up with a jerk of the swing. She took a couple of hollow steps across the porch, raised her hand to shield her eyes from the sun. Matt's face was in shadow, the brim of his Stetson pulled well down. But she knew without him having to say a word what had happened.

He crossed the yard at snail's pace, put one foot on the porch step, then stopped. Unable to meet Kirstie's burning gaze, he grasped the handrail and let his head sink forward.

"Moonshine," Kirstie whispered. Not a question, a terrible statement of fact. "He didn't make it."

There were a few things people always said when an animal you loved died.

"Never mind, honey. It's something you have to get used to."

"You did everything you could. He wouldn't have suffered."

"Remember, it's not the same as when a person dies."

"You'll soon get over it."

It was the last one that Kirstie hated the most. She would yell at any person dumb enough to say that. In fact, after Lisa had left for Lone Elm, Kirstie had avoided going out of the house all day, just so no one could try it. Come evening, as it grew dark and there was less risk of bumping in to anyone, she grabbed her hat and headed for the door.

"Where are you going?" Sandy asked. She'd driven back from Denver with a bunch of new guests to be greeted by the sad news about Moonshine. It had upset her almost as much as Kirstie and Matt, but she'd had to press on. There were cabins to allocate, late arrivals to check in, a hundred and one tasks to make changeover day run as smoothly as it ought. But now at last she had time to talk.

"Out to Red Fox Meadow," Kirstie told her.

"It's too late to ride." Her mom followed her to the door and looked out at the bands of dark clouds gathering over Eagle's Peak. The rest of the sky was indigo tinged in the west with pink.

"I know." Kirstie made out a group of new guests walking down the track from Apache Hill. Their flashlight gave off a weak yellow beam as they found their way toward the barbecue set out on the grass by Five Mile Creek. "I don't plan to ride," she told Sandy hastily. If she ran to the meadow, she would avoid the suppertime mob. "I just want to say hi to Lucky."

57

"Don't stay out too long!"

"OK, I won't." She swung out through the door, just catching her mom's last request.

"If you see Matt, tell him I'd like to talk with him!"

But Matt was one of the people Kirstie would rather avoid. She hadn't seen her brother all afternoon, knew only that he'd volunteered to drive Lisa to her grandpa's and that he hadn't been back to the ranch since. He was probably driving the back roads or hanging out in San Luis, trying not to think too hard about Moonshine.

In any case, she succeeded in skirting around the corral, then crossed the footbridge and slipped past the barbecue without being noticed. She could see the meadow fence up ahead and the dark outlines of horses quietly grazing.

As she approached and leaned on the fence, she picked out Yukon, the brown and white paint, with her black colt, Pepper. A little further off, pulling hay out of the sides of the metal feeder, were Matt's big gray horse, classy Cadillac and ugly old Crazy Horse. The two geldings went everywhere together and were recognizable at a glance.

More horses milled around in the dusk light

by the edge of the creek, wandering between willow bushes or nudging each other aside. Yeah, there was Jitterbug, dancing about as usual. And Johnny Mohawk, setting off to lope the length of the field.

But where was Lucky? It was odd for him not to be here by the fence. Usually he would hear and smell her even before she came into sight. His beautiful golden head would be stretching out to greet her, making her feel she was the most important thing in his world.

Yep, there he was, standing under an oak tree at the far end of the meadow. Kirstie spotted his pale mane, and recognized his trot as he set off toward her, the way he picked his feet high off the ground and arched his neck like an Arab, instead of the plain old quarter horse that he was. She smiled as she watched him approach. After this awful day, all she wanted to do was stand with him and talk.

"Hey!" she said quietly as he made his way past Cadillac and Crazy Horse.

He tossed his head and swished his tail, slowing to a walk. Then he plodded the last few yards, head down.

"Hey!" Kirstie said again. She climbed the fence and dropped into the meadow, feeling a few drops of rain in the cool breeze blowing down the valley. "Are you feeling like me, Lucky? All washed up."

Coming right up to her, he thrust his nose against her shoulder, licking her shirt and pulling at the pocket with his lips.

"I know!" she sighed. "We didn't get to go out together today, did we? You missed me, huh?"

More rubbing and licking, a sideways nudge as if to tell her off for neglecting him.

"I couldn't help it!" she grinned. "I was busy in the barn. We had a big problem which didn't work out too good. Tough, eh?"

Lucky snorted and pressed for more affection, almost making Kirstie overbalance in his eagerness.

"Listen, you got a day off, didn't you?" Hooking both arms around his neck, she laid her head against him. "And tomorrow's Monday, but I don't have to leave the ranch. It's vacation. School's out for summer!"

The palomino turned his head to look up at the black horizon, his nostrils flared, ears pricked.

"Yeah, you got it! We can ride all day, go where we want. What do you think? Should we try Eden Lake or Miners' Ridge? If we go to the lake you can take a swim!"

Giving another toss of his head, Lucky nickered.

"Yeah, I know; you like swimming. Me, too. But maybe Eden Lake's too far. You looked a little slow coming across the meadow just now, like you could do with taking things easy for a day or two."

Taking a step back from her horse, Kirstie cast a critical eye over him. She noticed he wasn't standing square on all four feet, but resting his left hind leg off the ground. Maybe he had a stone in his foot that was giving him a problem. So she went to lift and inspect the hoof in what was by now almost total darkness. "Nope, it looks fine!" she muttered, easing it back down. She went back around to his head and took hold of his head collar. "Hey, you're not kidding me, are you?"

Lucky shook himself, sending his whole body quivering. Then he gave a short, sharp cough.

It's nothing, Kirstie told herself. *Nothing! Lucky's fooling around, that's all.* She patted him and told him to quit, said she would go straight back to the ranch for her chicken and fries if he didn't behave. But that was on the surface. Deep down, she was growing afraid.

Take a proper look, an inner voice insisted. *It's not like Lucky to stand uneven. And he's low in energy. When did he last trot across the meadow to see you instead of lope?*

Take a look tomorrow! Another, high-pitched voice inside her head argued. *Leave it for tonight.*

Tomorrow could be too late. If there's something wrong with the horse, he needs proper attention now!

What could be wrong? Lucky's a strong, healthy horse. The whining voice wanted to be right.

Caught between the two, Kirstie couldn't move. She stood in Red Fox Meadow in the dark, with the rain coming down hard. Lucky had hung his head and was waiting quietly, but still the battle inside her head continued.

If it hadn't been for Matt coming up to the fence and seeing her there, she might have stayed all night. He stood silently for a few seconds, hat pulled down, jacket collar turned up, hands in pockets. "You OK?" he said at last.

"Fine." She shivered as the rain soaked through her shirt. The hand clutching the head collar shook with cold.

"How about Lucky?"

"Fine, too. Why shouldn't he be?" That was the whining, practically hysterical voice taking over.

"No, he's not." Matt climbed the fence to join them. He put his hand on the horse's shivering shoulder and looked him over from head to foot. "The horse is sick. C'mon, Kirstie, let's get him out of here!"

5

"Try not to let it get to you," Sandy told Kirstie, holding her hand hard. "I can see in your face you're thinking the worst already. But don't, honey. Think positive for Lucky's sake!"

Kirstie had walked her palomino out of the meadow to the barn. Cold rain and hot tears had trickled down her face as she led him slowly across the footbridge over Five Mile Creek, and she'd met her mom clearing up the rapidly removed remains of the Sunday evening barbecue. Reluctantly she'd handed Lucky over to Matt, who was bedding him down in a clean stall right this minute.

Sandy made her go into the house to dry off. She gave her a towel for her hair and fresh clothes from the closet. Kirstie went through the motions without saying a word.

"Hey, listen!" her mom insisted gently. "You know what we say when things get a little tough around here?"

She nodded, but the lump in her throat wouldn't let her speak.

"You gotta cowboy-up!" Sandy chanted the Half Moon Ranch mantra. "When the weather turns real cold and we get snow on the trail three feet deep, we keep right on trucking. A horse loses a shoe at nine thousand feet up on Eagle's Peak Trail, what do we do?"

"We cowboy-up," Kirstie answered faintly. For once, she was glad to be treated like a little kid. She liked the comfort of her mom's arm around her shoulder and the soft look in her kind gray eyes.

"Sure we do. And it's no different now that Lucky's sick. Look, you've known this guy for how many years?"

"Five." Sandy, together with Kirstie's grandpa, had bought the palomino as a one-year-old, soon after Sandy, Kirstie, and Matt had come to live at the ranch. Kirstie had been watching from her bedroom window when they'd brought him over from San Luis Sale Barn and opened up the back of the trailer. The youngster had practically tumbled down the ramp on his skinny legs, looking dazed and confused after the rough journey. He had been real cute as he kicked out and bucked, then took in his new surroundings. And the thing that had hit Kirstie between the eyes, that had set Lucky apart from any other colt she'd ever seen, was his amazing color.

Bright as new gold. They always said that about palominos, but with Lucky it was true. He shone, he glowed, he gleamed. He was like a lucky dollar. Her own lucky charm. Lucky.

"Five years," Sandy repeated. "And would you say he's weak or strong?"

"Strong." There was no trail he couldn't climb, no river he couldn't swim. They'd survived floods and landslides, gone everywhere together.

"Yeah. And what about willpower? Would you say he had a little or a lot?" Kirstie's mom finished drying her hair for her, then put a mug of chocolate in her cold hands.

"A lot." Kirstie didn't call it willpower; she called it courage. Lucky was the bravest horse she knew.

"Good. And he's smart, yeah?"

She nodded. Strong, brave, and clever. It was a great combination. It was what made her love him.

"So, trust him to get through this, whatever it is," Sandy advised, allowing Kirstie to take just one gulp of her hot drink then head for the door.

Halfway across the porch, Kirstie paused and turned. "Thanks, Mom!" She managed a brave half-smile before she rushed on across the dark, wet yard toward the barn.

"Take a look in his eyes." Matt showed Kirstie the telltale signs that her horse was sick. "Pull back the lid. You see the lining membrane? It should be a good, deep pink color."

Lucky's was pale, almost white. "So?" she asked.

"He's anemic. His temperature's over a hundred, and his resting pulse is forty-five."

"OK, he's sick," Kirstie agreed. "But it can't be equine flu; he had his shots last month."

"Yeah, that's what's so weird." Matt ran his hands over Lucky, feeling for swellings in the abdomen. "The symptoms are the same as Moonshine's, but the diagnosis has to be different. I'm thinking along the lines of a fever brought on by poisoning of some kind. Has Lucky been eating anything he shouldn't?"

"No way!" Kirstie was always on her guard. She never let him near any painted fences that might contain creosote or lead. And Red Fox Meadow was clear of plants that were dangerous to horses.

Matt frowned and stood up. "So maybe it's a worm infestation. They get parasites in the gut: red worm larvae, lungworm, whatever..."

More long words. She turned sharply and walked up to him, eyeball to eyeball. "How would that happen? Come on, how?"

"Hey!" Matt backed off, hands raised in surrender. "Don't shoot!"

"Sorry." Kirstie shook her head. "It bugs me, that's all, not knowing what's making him sick."

"OK, me, too. Let's think this thing through: a horse can ingest—eat—the larvae via grass. They damage the gut lining and cause infection. They can even get into the blood vessels and cut off the blood flow. That gives a horse bad colic. He gets a potbelly, anemia. But that's not the problem here, I guess..." Matt's frown deepened, then he dug into his kit for a stethoscope. "Did you notice Lucky coughing at all?"

Kirstie took a sharp breath. "Once or twice maybe." Why hadn't she paid any attention at the time, she wondered. Why had she been so busy worrying about Moonshine and neglecting her own horse? She waited while Matt listened to Lucky's chest.

And as she stood anxiously in the pool of yellow light cast by the overhead bulb, she heard footsteps and saw her mom and Hadley come into the barn. Their wet jackets and hats showed that it was still raining outside, and their quiet voices told Kirstie that they, too, were concerned.

"What's new?" Hadley asked as he drew near Lucky's stall.

Matt straightened up and let the stethoscope dangle from his neck. "Lungs don't sound too good," he told them. "There's a mucous discharge from the nose, too."

The wrangler nodded abruptly, leaning over the stall door for a closer look at the patient. "Listen, I heard Glen Woodford's out of town for a day or two, so how about you giving him penicillin to clear up the discharge?"

Under the circumstances, Matt agreed to use the ranch's own antibiotics. "We can give him 30ccs of procaine twice a day to see if it helps. Plus a shot or two of benzathine into the muscle."

"And how long do we rest him?"

"Seven days minimum."

Kirstie listened without taking in the details. It bothered her that Hadley, with a lifetime of dealing with horses behind him, had only needed one quick look to decide that the situation was serious.

Perhaps it was Lucky's body language that sent a strong message. He'd backed off into a dark corner of the stall, head hanging, so unlike his usual inquisitive self that he hardly looked like the same horse.

"Let's leave him to get some rest," Sandy suggested after the men had stopped talking and a tense silence had developed. She led the way toward the barn door, while overhead the rain fell steadily on the corrugated tin roof.

For a while, Kirstie held back. She checked the bedding, the water feeder, reluctant to turn off the light and leave Lucky in darkness.

"Kirstie?" Sandy called.

One last look, trying to convince herself that he wasn't as sick as they were making out, that his coat wasn't so dull, his eyes not so lifeless as they might think. It was the way the shadows fell, a trick of the light.

From the far corner Lucky stared back at her. His pale mane hung lank over his face; he made no effort to move.

"Kirstie!" A more insistent call from her mom.

"Coming!" Quickly she switched off the light above the stall and plunged the barn into total darkness.

Monday, the first day of June, dawned bright and clear, with little sign of the rain of the night before. When Kirstie looked out of her window, Eagle's Peak basked in early morning sunlight, and the sky was a delicate bird's egg blue.

It was a day when she would normally call Lisa

and say, "Come ride up to Eden Lake with me. You take Rodeo Rocky. (No need to say that she, Kirstie, would be riding Lucky.) We'll make a sack lunch, take swimming stuff, and stay out the whole day!"

Lisa would answer in a sleepy voice from her bedroom above the End of Trail Diner in San Luis. "Jeez, Kirstie, do you know what time it is? It's six thirty, for heaven's sakes! This is a vacation. Just give me a break!"

But she would put down the phone, pull a comb through her wavy hair, stick on a T-shirt and jeans, then grab a lift from a truck driver friend of her mom's taking breakfast in the diner. She would show up at Half Moon Ranch still grumbling about a girl needing her beauty sleep. It would be 8 a.m., time for a ranch breakfast of blueberry pancake and maple syrup. "Too many calories!" Lisa would protest, stuffing Hershey bars and marshmallows in with her sack lunch. "Say, these are new jeans. Do they make me look fat?"

Meltwater Trail would beckon: a game of Find the Flag with a new bunch of dude riders. Then on out of the stands of fresh green aspens, between tall

72

lodgepole pines standing sentry along the high tracks leading to the bare ridges of pink granite to Bear Hunt Overlook, Elk Rock, and Dead Man's Canyon. And beyond that the snow line. The glittering, ice-bound shores of Eden Lake. The two girls and their horses would enter a silent, shining paradise.

But today was different. No phone calls. No leaving her cares behind. Today Kirstie's only thought was to get over to the barn to see how Lucky was.

Matt was already out there with Charlie, telling the young wrangler to feed the patient small amounts of molasses and concentrates throughout the day. "No oats," he reminded him. "Dissolve the procaine tablets in his drinking water. And keep his bedding clean, OK?"

"I'll do it," Kirstie volunteered, going into the stall. She could see that Lucky was no better, and that this time she couldn't blame the artificial light for the dull look of his lovely golden coat. "Is it OK if I groom him?"

"Sure." Matt was moving off with Charlie. "But don't handle him too much. He most likely wants some peace."

Like a person with flu, she guessed. A horse's bones would ache; he'd be feeling stiff in his joints and tired to death. So she took a soft brush and worked him over from head to foot, talking to him soothingly as she covered him with a light blanket and reached under his belly to fasten the straps. He stood patiently, taking little interest in what she did.

"OK, I'm done," she assured him. "Now you get some rest. I'll be back in a couple of hours."

Leaving him in the cramped stall, head hanging, looking tired and sad, she went off to help Charlie saddle up the horses for the day's trail rides. She bridled them up, checked cinches, divided riders into beginners, intermediates, and advanced, and saw them on their way.

"How come you're not riding today?" Hadley called as he headed the intermediates out across Five Mile Creek.

Kirstie shrugged. "I need to take care of Lucky."

"You sure, honey?" Sandy checked, looking down from the saddle, the low sun behind her making her fair hair shine like a halo. Her ride was with the beginners, up Apache Hill and along Coyote Trail.

"Yeah. I want to be here for him."

"OK. Charlie's gonna be in the maintenance area this morning, servicing the truck and trying to get in touch with Glen Woodford to check if he's on his way. Ask him for help if you need it."

Listless and heavyhearted, Kirstie saw off the group of excited, nervous riders. Even before they'd reached the top of Apache Hill, she was already wanting to run back and check on Lucky, having to tell herself firmly that the poor guy needed to sleep. So she wandered aimlessly into the tack room instead and began shooing cats and sweeping the floor just to keep herself occupied. The one black and two gray kittens kept on coming back and pouncing on the broom, tumbling out of the way, then scooting in and out of the door.

"Hey, kitties!" a light, cheerful voice said.

"Lisa!" Kirstie put down the broom and went outside. Her best friend was picking up the black kitten and tickling him under his chin. "How come?"

"What do you mean, 'How come?' It's our vacation, isn't it? It's me who should be asking 'How come?' How come you didn't call me at some dreadful time this morning?"

Kirstie blushed, then frowned. "Lucky's sick."

"Yeah. Charlie just told me." Lisa put down the kitten and gave her a long, hard look. "So? How come you didn't call?"

"I should've, I guess. Sorry."

Lisa stepped out into the corral, put her hands on her hips, and went on with her lecture. "Let me guess. You feel bad because you rescued the appie and the appie gave Moonshine and Lucky the flu..."

"Lucky didn't catch the bug!" Kirstie cut in quickly. "We can't get hold of Glen and we don't know what his problem is!"

Lisa nodded. "OK. It's not the flu, but somehow you still feel it's your fault." She put up her hand to ward off another interruption. "Yeah, you do. I know you, Kirstie. Guilt, guilt, guilt. It's written all over your face. And look at you; you didn't even comb your hair this morning!"

"Lisa, give me a break." This wasn't what Kirstie needed. She turned away, planning to retreat into the tack room.

"But where did guilt ever get you?" Lisa insisted. She leaped ahead of Kirstie, barring her way. "You gotta get it into your skull that horses get sick without it being your fault. Think about it a different way."

"Like what?" Kirstie couldn't take much more of this. She could feel the stupid tears welling up again.

"Like, what can we do now? What's gonna be the best thing to help Lucky get better?"

"You mean, cowboy-up?" Kirstie's voice was low and scornful. "Spare me, Lisa. I already had that from Mom."

"Yeah, cowboy-up!" Lisa's green eyes sparked. She refused to back off. "Think. Make plans. If Matt's stymied and can't work out what's wrong with Lucky, and you're really afraid it's something serious, then get a move on!"

"And do what?" Gosh, if she could think of something useful to do, instead of feeling totally helpless every time she so much as looked at Lucky, didn't Lisa think she would do it?

"Get a second opinion!" her friend insisted. "Don't hang around. Call Glen Woodford again!"

* * *

"Lucky's running a high fever, that's for sure."

Kirstie and Lisa stayed in the background with Tommy Woodford as Glen talked Lucky's case through with Matt. The vet had finally been contacted shortly after Sandy Scott had returned from her morning ride.

"And there's a respiratory problem that we need to check out."

"How're we gonna do that?" Sandy asked. She'd assured Glen that the cost of getting the palomino back to full health wasn't an issue. "Whatever it takes," she'd insisted. "Never mind the expense."

"First, we make a culture of the nasal discharge and look for bacterial infection. We'll be looking for a herpes virus, say. That would fit in with a slight swelling I can feel beneath the horse's jaw."

As she listened to the technical stuff, Kirstie felt a little better. Glen sure knew what he was talking about. Not that Matt didn't, but the vet from San Luis had years of experience in treating sick horses.

"If it's herpes, all you need to do is rest Lucky until the infection clears up. Period."

Lisa nudged Kirstie's arm and smiled.

"If we find equine influenza, that's more serious," Glen went on.

"It's not that!" Kirstie quickly reminded them about the up-to-date health program. "You vaccinated Lucky yourself, remember!"

"OK, so the other options include a streptococcus virus, so we have to watch out for abscesses under the jaw. Or else it could be emphysema: lung damage caused by an allergy to spores in mold that you get around fodder and bedding."

By this time, Kirstie found that the long words had begun to have the reverse effect. Instead of being reassured by Glen's knowledge, she felt scared by the number of serious illnesses a horse could get. And now he was moving on to an examination of the inside of Lucky's airways which involved pushing a tube through his nostril, down the windpipe into his lungs.

"The tube contains fiber optic strands," Glen explained. "They're connected to this light source so we get to see the damage to the lungs, if any."

As the vet approached Lucky with the tube, Kirstie backed away from the stall in dismay. She didn't want to stay to see this, so she walked out of the barn, leaving the cluster of experts—her mom, Matt, and Glen—to carry out the examination. Lisa chose to watch, her face tense, her jaw clenched tight. But Tommy followed Kirstie out into the daylight.

"Jeez!" Closing her eyes, she leaned against the wall of the barn and took a deep breath. The wooden boards felt warm through her thin cotton shirt.

Tommy walked ahead a few paces, then kicked his toe against a tethering post. His mouth was screwed up tight and he gave a slight shake of his head. "Kirstie…"

"What?" She opened her eyes to squint into the sun at the hunched figure in a black T-shirt and jeans.

"I got something to tell you." More uneasy than ever, he scuffed his boot in the dust.

"I'm not gonna like it, am I?" Pushing herself free of the wall, she edged toward him. Tommy was so quiet it was unusual for him to begin a conversation. He was just someone who was always there in the background, helping his dad with the paperwork that all vets carried with them.

"It's about Lucky's flu shot." He paused, sighed, then forced himself to carry on. "The file for April shows that we gave all the Half Moon Ranch horses their booster for tetanus, influenza, and rhino..."

"Yeah?" They'd looked at the files when Moonshine fell ill. All the boxes had check marks filled in. "So?"

"The list ain't right," Tommy told her. He left off scuffing his boot and looked up at her with hooded eyes.

"How come?"

"It ain't true that all the horses had their shots. I was the one checking them off, so I should know!"

"Meaning what exactly?" At times like this, when new possibilities exploded inside her head, she asked the dumbest questions.

"Meaning, we needed to get out of here fast, onto the next job. My pa gives the shots; I line up the horses and check them off the list. He deals with so many, he don't remember the names of each and every horse. That's my job."

Kirstie clenched her fists and practically stopped breathing. What was Tommy building up to?

"So what I did when we ran short of time was look at a few horses way down the list: Cadillac, Moose, Crazy Horse, and Lucky. I see it's only ninety days since we gave them the last booster, and I reckon there's not much risk if we just leave them off the list that day, so long as I keep it in my head to put them at the top of the list next time."

"But you put a check mark in the box to make it look as if we were up to date?" Another dumb question, but Kirstie found it hard to believe what Tommy was telling her.

He nodded, unable to look her in the eye any longer.

"So Lucky didn't have the shot, which means right now he isn't immune to tetanus…"

"Or rhinopneumonitis…"

"Or influenza!" she gasped. "Oh, my gosh, Tommy, why didn't you tell us this before?"

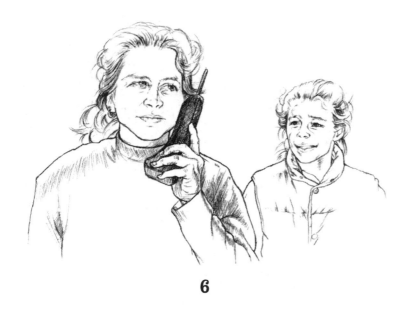

6

It was like fitting a new piece in a difficult jigsaw, the fact that Lucky and several other horses at Half Moon Ranch had been left wide open to infection.

"Horse flu is what killed Moonshine!" Kirstie walked with Lisa up and down the ranch house porch. "It turns into pneumonia and kills them. At the very least, they have permanent damage to their lungs!"

"Wait!" Lisa's advice was brief. She'd watched and listened hard as Tommy had come back into the barn after his talk with Kirstie to confess what he'd done.

"How can I? Like, waiting is the last thing we should do. Didn't we lose enough time already?" Kirstie meant the hours lost because of Tommy's guilty silence.

"Look, Glen did all the tests and took them off to the lab, didn't he? Now we just have to hang on until he gets the results."

"It's flu," Kirstie said in a flat, fatalistic voice, her face marked by a grim frown. "I feel that's what it is. Lucky was the one who got closest of all to Whisper. The pony was coughing those bugs all over him."

"Say you're right." Lisa caught her arm to stop her pacing up and down. "It's still good nursing and a whole lot of patience that's gonna pull Lucky through."

Kirstie broke free and stepped down into the yard. Over in the corral, guests were gathering for the afternoon rides. The routine of the ranch carried on regardless. "It's weird!" She turned back to Lisa. "We got all these tests and drugs with fancy, scientific names; we got labs and hospitals for horses and all the modern stuff, but we still can't do a single thing to help Lucky!"

Matt had tried and Glen Woodford was doing his best, but still no one was certain what was wrong. And the thing everyone told her was "Wait and see."

"There must be something else!" she insisted.

"Yeah, modern stuff..." Lisa echoed. Knitting her brows and catching her bottom lip between her teeth, she stepped down absentmindedly from the porch, staring at Hadley who was in the corral helping riders to mount their horses.

"Here we are, the turn of the millennium, living in a country with the most up-to-date Western medicines you could wish for, and they say 'Rest.' That's it! 'Rest' and 'Wait and see'!" Kirstie's impatience took her across the yard toward the corral, to lean on the fence.

Lisa joined her. "Uhmm ... Kirstie..."

"Yeah?" Once the rides were out of the way, her plan was to help Charlie dissolve Lucky's next dose of penicillin in his drinking water.

"...Say we stopped thinking modern here. Say we started thinking something more traditional." Lisa spoke slowly and quietly, without her usual bubbling self-confidence. She was still staring thoughtfully at the senior wrangler.

Puzzled, Kirstie followed her line of vision. "No use asking Hadley," she objected before Lisa could even suggest it. "He already said that the type of infection Lucky's got is bad news. 'The ruin of many a good saddle horse,' to use his words." The old man had looked in on Lucky over lunch and more or less written him off.

"I wasn't thinking of asking Hadley's advice." Lisa sniffed and climbed the fence. She headed for the lean, slightly stooped figure of the longest serving member of the Half Moon Ranch crew. "It's his brains I'm interested in. Pure information, honest!"

Kirstie clicked out of her gloomy mood and followed, weaving between horses and riders, avoiding Charlie's long rake as it cleared the yard.

"Hey, Hadley!" Lisa looked up at him as he settled in the saddle on Silver Flash, his hat pulled well down, a blue neckerchief protecting the back of his neck from the sun. "You remember a guy called Red Mitchell who worked here way back?"

"Uh-huh." Hadley backed his sorrel horse

away from the post, one eye on the group of advanced riders.

"That means, 'Uh-huh; yep'?" Lisa reached for Silver Flash's rein.

A nod, a shrug, so what?

"He had a horse called Bandit?"

"Black-and-white paint," came the swift reply. Hadley was always more interested in talking about horses than about people. "That gelding had great presence: part Morgan, part quarter horse. Never lost his cool, most hardworking cutter you ever seen."

"That's the one!" Lisa stole a quick glance at Kirstie to see if she was clued in. "OK, so Red Mitchell took Bandit to some horse doctor when he fell sick one year." She recounted the story her grandpa had told her.

"Yep." Hadley clammed up again, making it clear he didn't have time to chat.

"This horse doctor; where did he hang out?" Refusing to let go of Silver Flash's rein, Lisa followed Hadley across the corral.

"In the mountains, way out West, I forget."

"In Colorado? Wyoming? Montana?"

"Montana." Hadley saw that he wouldn't get rid of Lisa until he'd given her some answers. "Long way from here. Place called Rainbow Mountain."

"And when was this?" Lisa realized her time was running out. Hadley's group had surrounded him, eager to leave. "Twenty years back? Thirty? What was the guy's name, do you remember?"

"Twenty, twenty-five years. I didn't pay too much attention. All I know is, Red Mitchell got some damn fool idea into his head that his sick horse needed special medicine from a guy holed up in the mountains. Had some Native American blood, as I recall. Sioux maybe, or Comanche."

Lisa nodded eagerly, storing the information for future reference. "His name!" she pleaded.

Hadley raked through his memory one last time. "Maybe it was Stone. Zak Stone. Yeah, I guess that was it."

"Hang on just a minute!" Sandy Scott had trouble taking in Kirstie's eager plan. She'd returned from her afternoon ride to find her daughter transformed. Instead of a listless, anxious wreck, she'd been greeted by this energetic blonde whirlwind. "Tell me one more time!"

"Zak Stone!" Kirstie repeated the name. "Lisa and me asked Hadley about him. Then we called all the old-timers on the ranches around here!"

"You've been running up my phone bill, huh?" Her mom refused to be drawn in. Instead, she poured herself a cup of coffee.

"Grandpa couldn't recall much more than Hadley," Lisa reported. "But Jim Mullins at Lazy B said everyone knew about Zak Stone in those days. He had a name as the best horse doctor in the West."

"So how come I never heard of him?" Sandy sat down wearily at the table.

"Because he's a hermit!" Kirstie jumped back in. "You know; he don't."

" 'Doesn't'!" Sandy corrected.

"He doesn't like having folks around. Lives in the backwoods on Rainbow Mountain in south east Montana. If people want to see him, they gotta find their own way. You could drive for days across country, I guess, and turn up at his place without knowing for sure that you'd find him home."

"Very convenient!" Sandy looked up at Matt, who had just come in, with a sigh that said "Help!"

"Find who home?" Kirstie's brother asked. He too looked dead beat.

"Zak Stone!" Kirstie began the explanations all over again. "Part Sioux...old, Native American remedies...herbs and stuff...works like magic... holed up in the mountains of Montana!"

"And all this is over twenty years back," Sandy stressed. "He hasn't even been heard of in these parts for at least five years. So forget it, Matt. And Kirstie, don't even think what I think you're thinking about!"

"The best in the West!" Kirstie repeated.

It was late evening. She and Matt stood in the barn, gazing quietly into Lucky's stall. The only sounds were the whispering rustles of hidden, small creatures creeping through the hay or perched on rafters, and the painful rasps of Lucky's lungs as he struggled to draw breath.

"Yeah, but logically, Mom's got a point." Matt had a foot in each camp; he saw that the Zak Stone option might be a straw to clutch at, but equally he agreed with Sandy that it was at best a long shot as far as finding a cure for Lucky went.

In…out, in and out again. Kirstie stared at the difficult, double lift of Lucky's ribcage as he breathed out through the blocked airways. "What's logic got to do with it?" she whispered.

"Sandy? Lennie Goodman here."

Kirstie had picked up the phone early next morning, thinking it might be Glen Woodford with Lucky's test results. "Hi, Lennie. This is Kirstie. Mom's right here."

She handed over the phone and stuck around, hearing the mild surprise in Sandy's voice and her repetition of Lisa's grandpa's words.

"Zak Stone? Not that name again!" Kirstie's mom tried to make light of the question that had been hanging over the family all night. "My crazy daughter's half persuaded my sane son that driving a truck across America with a sick horse to see a Sioux horse doctor who might not even be alive after all these years is a good idea!"

Kirstie caught sight of Matt through the window and beckoned him inside. "Shh!" she warned, her finger to her lips, as the phone conversation continued.

"Lennie, you surprise me!" Sandy laughed. "Here's me thinking you were on my side. And what do I get? More Zak Stone! OK, so you recall hearing Red Mitchell sing this man's praises. But that was then. This is now. How come you get behind this hippy stuff?"

Holding her breath, thanking Lisa for convincing Lennie to make the call, since no doubt it had been her friend's idea, she prayed that Sandy would sway their way.

"So, you hear Mr. Stone's still living in his hermit hideaway on Rainbow Mountain?" She cupped her hand over the phone and raised her eyebrows at her son. "Can you believe this?"

Matt shrugged.

"How's Lucky?" Kirstie whispered, realizing that he'd just come from the barn.

He shook his head and turned away.

"…OK, Lennie, I'll think about it. Thanks for the call." Sandy put down the phone, staring thoughtfully out of the window.

"What's to think about?" Kirstie began. *Please,*

please, please let me do this! she begged silently. *Give Lucky a chance!*

"Matt?" Her mom glanced up at last. The look on her face said she was at a loss.

At first he didn't reply. The silence seemed to go on forever. "The horse is pretty weak. I don't know for sure that he could stand the journey," he began slowly.

"And are you certain that there's nothing either you or Glen can do for him if we keep him here?" Sandy double checked all the possibilities. Her gaze drifted to Kirstie's face, held by her intense stare.

Matt shook his head. "We've drawn two blanks," he admitted. "Even with Glen's test results to identify the infection, if that's what it is, there still ain't a lot we can give him."

Two blanks. Two failures. *Please, please give him a third chance!*

"You want to take him to Montana?" Sandy asked.

"I guess," Matt agreed quietly.

Yes! Kirstie closed her eyes. *Third-time lucky! It has to be!*

Tuesday, midday, Lucky was loaded in a truck borrowed from Lennie Goodman, who'd driven it

straight over from Lone Elm the moment Sandy had agreed to the plan. The horse had gone in without protest, too weak and ill to take in much about his change of surroundings. His coat, wringing wet across the shoulders and withers, was dull and lifeless, his legs and beautiful flowing tail bandaged tight for the journey.

"Easy, boy!" Kirstie whispered and cajoled him into position, tying him firmly so that he didn't come to harm when the truck swayed and jolted along the narrow country roads.

Lucky looked back at her with a passive, uninterested stare. No spark, no pleasure in her gentle touch. Nothing.

"We're gonna get you better. Trust me." If ever she'd wanted him to understand her words it was now. But then maybe he did know what her hands and eyes told him. In any case, he stood patiently in the stall inside the truck, waiting for the journey to begin.

"I'm not gonna make a big deal," Sandy told Kirstie and Matt as she helped bolt the ramp into place then saw them into the cab. "That's what moms do at times like this, so I won't!"

Still, there was a worried crease between her eyes, and a sack full of tinned beans, chips, and chocolate bars that she'd prepared, now tucked safely between Kirstie's feet. And she'd already asked them three times over about money, motels, cell phone, and maps.

"OK, no big deal!" Kirstie agreed.

Matt started the engine, checked the fuel gauge, and leaned out of his side of the cab for a few final words with Charlie about the possible temperamental aspects of Lennie's elderly diesel truck, since their own was still laid up in the maintenance shed.

Kirstie caught sight of Lisa standing quietly on the house porch with her grandpa. "Why don't you come?" she mouthed, for at least the third time.

"…Come with us!" she'd begged. "This whole thing was your idea. Why not come along?"

"No way!" Lisa had made a million excuses: she didn't like riding in trucks, Bonnie needed her in the diner, she had ten thousand and one more interesting things planned.

"So what's the real reason?" Kirstie had pressed her for an answer she could believe.

"This is your trip," Lisa had replied. "Yours and Matt's and Lucky's."

And she'd stuck to that, even now, when her face was wistful, her hair blown about by the breeze that had got up since breakfast. She came down from the porch as Matt eased the truck into gear.

"Map?" she asked.

Kirstie held it up for her to see.

"Address?"

"Zak Stone, Somewhere on Rainbow Mountain, Wentworth County, Montana!" She recited with a grin what little they knew.

Lisa nodded and smiled. "So, give me a call."

Kirstie's turn to nod and wave.

"Safe journey!" Sandy called.

Lisa held two hands in the air, a double wave. "Good luck!"

The truck rolled out of the yard up the drive. It rattled across the cattle guard and lurched around the first stiff bend. That was it; Half Moon Ranch was out of sight. Lucky, Matt, and Kirstie were on the road.

7

They drove north on the Interstate around Denver, then took a highway that led west through the Rocky Mountain National Park. Trail Ridge Road took them to a height of 12,000 feet into a world of ice and snow. Glaciers glinted on Flatiron Mountain and Nakai Peak. The narrow road switchbacked through steep valleys across the roof of America.

"You see those peaks ahead?" Matt pointed into the distance. It was late afternoon, four hours into the two-day journey. "I reckon they're the Never Summer Mountains."

"Are you serious?"

"Yeah. The Never Summer Mountains. How's it sound to you?"

"Great!" Though the cab was warm, Kirstie shivered. She leaned forward to turn up the volume on the radio. A guitar sobbed Western-style notes, while a country singer gave them the tearful story of a woman he had loved and lost. "Where do we plan to spend the night? Don't tell me: Frozen Fingers Ridge, Dead Man's Wilderness, Eaten-By-Bears Lodge!"

Matt grinned and took a hairpin bend. "I take it you're not grabbed by the amazing alpine landscape, Ms. Scott?"

"Jeez, Matt slow down!" Kirstie twisted sideways, then straightened up. "We've got a sick horse in the back, remember."

"How could I forget?" The reminder sobered him up anyway. "Listen, we'll be out of this snow pretty soon and heading for the Arapaho National Forest. We'll stay overnight in Kawuneeche Valley, get an early start tomorrow, and be across the Great Divide by midday."

As she listened to the plan, with the country

singer wailing in the background, Kirstie noticed soft white flecks whirl out of a darkening sky and land on the windshield. Soon, the road ahead was covered with a fine dusting of snow. "Oh, great!" she moaned again. "A blizzard in June—that's all we need!"

Ignoring her, Matt trucked on. The wipers whooshed and squeaked, keeping the screen clear; the engine whined and struggled with the gradients. Thirty minutes later they would be through the worst of the weather, he promised.

"I could've loved you better," the country and western star wailed. "Didn't mean to be unkind. You know that was the last thing on my mind!"

Kawuneeche Valley was green. Yellow, pink, and blue flowers spread across the hillsides like a huge, soft carpet, as far as the gray granite rocks. Beyond them were more mountains, more rugged and bigger still than the ones Kirstie and Matt had driven though on this, their first day on the road.

Matt pulled up in a small campground run by a forest ranger named Bill Englemann. The ranger, an elderly man with a paunch and a fine head of pure white hair, showed them where to build a wood fire for cooking. "Ain't nothing fancy here," he warned. "No showers, no telephones, no other campers using the site tonight—nothing except clean air and peace and quiet."

When he saw the palomino horse in the trailer and heard the reason why they were traveling northwest, Bill told Kirstie she could lead Lucky out of the trailer into a small, secluded pasture at the back of his cabin.

"You hear that?" Kirstie lowered the ramp and went inside the trailer to untie Lucky. She noticed that he'd eaten very little hay from his net and that his breathing was no easier than it had been when they'd set off from Half Moon Ranch. "You think you can make it out to Bill's meadow?" she cajoled, leading him carefully into the open.

Dragging his feet, Lucky slipped and slid down the ramp. His legs seemed stiff after the journey; his coat was patchy with sweat, his head hanging low.

"I got good clean water back here," the ranger told Kirstie in a concerned voice, leading the way around the side of his small log cabin.

"C'mon, boy!" she urged, feeling Lucky pull back. "I know you don't feel too good, and this is a pretty strange place for you to find yourself. Yeah, those are new mountains over there!"

Lucky had half raised his head and flared his nostrils. His ears came forward slightly as he took in his surroundings.

"You see that one with the sun on? I checked it out on the map. It's named Blue Ridge Mountain. The snow's beautiful, isn't it? Cold, but you gotta admit, it sure is pretty." She smiled as Lucky's head turned in the direction of her pointing finger. "We drive across to Blue Ridge at dawn tomorrow. After that, we go down into Wyoming. You know Wyoming? It's where your ancestors roamed the prairies—wild mustangs, thousands of them. You're gonna like Wyoming!"

The sound of her voice seemed to encourage him. He took a few stiff steps forward.

"She always talk to her horse?" Bill Englemann quizzed Matt, standing to one side to give Kirstie and Lucky room to pass. He closed the gate to the meadow after them.

"More than she talks to me!" Matt told him. He

went off to cook beans and make coffee while his sister settled Lucky down for the night.

"No point telling you not to worry?" Matt said quietly as he handed Kirstie her supper.

Sitting huddled inside a blanket at the opposite side of the fire, she sighed and shook her head.

The campfire flickered and glowed red. Overhead, the black sky was dotted with silver stars.

"So, eat!" Matt ordered.

She moved the beans around her plate with her fork. "I think Lucky got worse," she confessed. "He hardly ate anything all day. His breathing sounds real rough."

"He's bad," Matt admitted. "I ain't gonna pretend otherwise." With his solemn, handsome face shadowed by the dancing flames, he fell silent for a while. "On the bright side, it's been a couple of days now, and he's still hanging on in there."

Kirstie nodded miserably. "Matt, you should see how he looks at me. Like, he's asking me for help because he feels so bad. And he's wondering what's wrong—why he can't run around and act normal.

And when he doesn't get an answer, it's like I'm
letting him down big time!"

"You're not letting him down." Matt gazed at
her across the flames. "We're doing everything
we can."

"Not enough," she murmured. In a dark place
in her heart that she would never share, she hid a
gnawing fear that what they were doing now was
too little, too late. Lucky was going to die.

"Yeah!" Matt contradicted in a louder, firmer
voice. "Enough. We're doing plenty here. You gotta
believe that!"

"What exactly?" She stared back at him, startled into paying more attention.

Matt frowned. "Zak Stone was your idea, remember."

"Yeah, but what exactly are we letting Lucky in for when we get there?" Here, under the vast canopy of stars, with woodsmoke and sparks drifting skyward, she felt at a loss. What had seemed like a good idea when Lisa framed it had lost its focus. "What do we know about him?"

"Zak Stone?" Matt shrugged.

"Or about this medicine stuff he does?"

"It's Native American; we know that." Matt gathered together what little information they had. "OK, so that's gotta be about spirits and visions, stuff like that. Maybe herbs to help healing."

Spirits? Visions? Kirstie gazed up at the dancing red sparks. Her eyes were stinging from the smoke and from the tears that would keep on springing up. "Do you mean this is about ghosts?"

"Well, it sure ain't about antibiotics and endoscopes!" Matt told her. He stood up suddenly. "If you change your mind, we can turn the trailer around and head for home first thing tomorrow."

"I didn't change my mind!" Jolted by his quick turnaround, she, too, stood up. "Did you?"

They were face to face, doubt written over their features: Matt's dark and angular, Kirstie's fair and softer.

"We don't know enough to make a good decision," Matt pointed out. "We don't know what kind of healing is involved, except we can be pretty sure it's like nothing I ever learned in vet school. But, hey, we don't even know if this guy is gonna be there!"

Slowly she nodded. "We tried everything you and Glen knew before we set off, didn't we?"

"Everything."

"So it's more to do with how we feel." Like she'd said to him before, when they'd both taken this Zak Stone stuff on board: "What's logic got to do with it?"

"I guess."

"So, how do you feel?"

Matt's doubts intensified. He shook his head hard. "I think..."

"Not think, feel?"

"I feel scared," he admitted. "Like everything I learned about being a good vet might turn out to be garbage. How about you?"

"Scared, too," she whispered. "That Zak Stone will take one look at Lucky and say there's nothing he can do."

There was a million miles of space out there, planets so many light years away you couldn't begin to understand. A sprinkling of ancient light.

"So?" Kirstie asked Matt.

He looked up at the sky, then turned back to her. "We go onto Rainbow Mountain," he said.

On Wednesday morning they crossed the Great Divide, the jagged backbone of mountains that split the United States from north to south. West of the Rockies into Wyoming, the map gave Kirstie gentler names for the endless expanses of high, flat land: Sweetwater, Sandy River, and Pinedale.

"Keep going on Interstate 80 through Cheyenne and Laramie," Bill Englemann had instructed them. "Take a right at Rock Springs for Jackson and Teton National Park. You can't miss it."

"We're aiming for Montana," Matt had told the kind and courteous forest guard. "Rainbow Mountain, Wentworth County. Do you know it?"

"Sure." Bill had stabbed Kirstie's map with a stumpy forefinger. "Through Yellowstone, across the state border, still on the 80. You're pretty close to Bighorn Canyon where Custer made his Last Stand. There are a couple of reservations up that way, too: Cheyenne and Crow Indians."

"How long is the drive?" Matt had checked his watch at 7 a.m.

"Three hundred and fifty, four hundred miles, straight through the Cowboy State into the Big Sky!"

"Sounds good to me!" Kirstie had said as they set off.

By midmorning, they'd traveled a hundred and fifty of the four hundred miles and stopped twice to water Lucky. They'd seen road signs warning them of the presence in the area of elk, moose, and grizzlies and others inviting them to stop off and soak in half a dozen natural hot springs.

"Happy now?" Matt asked Kirstie. The flat plains stretched on forever, the white road straight as a die.

"I will be when we cross into Montana." Dipping her hand into the bag of provisions made up by their mom, she drew out a couple of apples and threw one to him. The radio played a cheerful, jog-along tune about cowboys rounding up cattle and singing around the campfire.

The sun rose in a clear sky; the land was empty and windswept. At midday Matt stopped for gas while Kirstie went to check on Lucky. She made him drink and eat a little alfalfa, promised him that by the following day they would have reached their journey's end. "Rainbow Mountain!" she whispered in his ear. "Sounds kinda nice, doesn't it?"

A listless Lucky nuzzled her hand, his lank mane brushing against her cheek.

"It will be," she said, resting her hand on his trembling neck. "And there's a guy up there who everybody talks about as the best horse doctor around. OK, so he's not your ordinary vet, with drugs and needles and stuff. He may be a little weird with his herbs and visions; who knows?"

Coming back from the gas station shop with ice cream and candy bars, Matt raised his eyebrows at her, kidding her as usual. "Talk about weird!"

"We'll ignore that!" Kirstie told Lucky. She checked his leg bandages, his head collar, his hay net. "All we need to think about is Rainbow Mountain and persuading Zak Stone to make you better, OK?"

In Montana you could see forever. Matt and Kirstie drove Lucky over the border early on Thursday morning. Hawks wheeled in the vast expanse of blue sky. The land to either side of the dirt road was dry, the grass brittle and dotted here and there with old red barns.

They'd broken camp at dawn, kicked earth over their still smoldering campfire, and washed in the cold clear water of a nearby stream. Kirstie had groomed Lucky, trying not to notice the dull, lifeless condition of his once beautiful golden coat. She'd forced a little more feed on him, knowing how difficult it must be for him to chew and swallow when she heard the choked struggling intake of air into his lungs and the noisy, coughing exhalation. "Soon!" she'd whispered as she'd bolted the ramp into position, ready for the final leg of the journey. "Trust me!"

She spent the morning in the passenger seat, tracing their way through the backcountry of southern

Montana, shoulders hunched over the creased map. By eleven o'clock they'd passed through a couple of ghost towns—empty wooden houses with boarded-up windows, defunct fuel pumps by the roadside, a rusting, overgrown railway line that stopped in the middle of nowhere. Still the birds circled overhead, while watery clouds were dragged across the blue sky by a wind from the east. By midday, the rain set in.

"Wentworth County." Matt read the sign by the side of the road.

Kirstie looked up from the map, through the greasy, insect-stained windshield. The wipers weren't doing a good job on the drizzle, but she could still make out hills like soft green pincushions in the distance, a change from the unbroken plains they'd been traveling through all morning. "The next place should be Bear Claw Creek, I guess."

Matt worked his stiff shoulders up and down. "I reckon that's where we stop to ask a few questions."

If the map was right, Bear Claw Creek was the last town before Rainbow Mountain and the only place where Kirstie and Matt would be likely to get information on Zak Stone. Suddenly, after the long, semi-dazed hours in the truck, Kirstie found herself sitting forward on the edge of her seat.

She noticed a covered wooden bridge over a creek to their left, two haystacks perched on the low horizon. Beyond them there was a farm with white specks moving about in the yard, geese perhaps. Then, on the dirt road ahead, were two cowboys on horseback, well used ropes looped around their saddle horns, weathered chaps flapping wetly against their horses' flanks.

As Matt passed the two riders, he leaned out of his window. "Bear Claw Creek?" he asked.

"Right up ahead," came the low, slow reply. "'Bout a mile. You can't hardly miss it!"

"…Yeah, there!" After a minute or two, Kirstie was able to point to two rows of houses lining the road. They looked dark and dismal through the misty rain, an impression made worse by a couple of old trucks without wheels dumped at the fringe of the town and a steel grain silo towering behind. The buildings dribbled on for a few hundred yards until Matt drove into the town center, a crossroads with telegraph wires looped overhead, a general store, a gas station, and an old cinema.

As he pulled over to the right and coasted into the gas station, Kirstie bit back her disappointment. This was nothing like the place she'd pictured. For miles of blue sky, read gray rain clouds. For pretty farms on green hillsides, read a run-down hick town in the middle of nowhere.

"Hey." Matt greeted the young woman who came out to serve gas.

Dark-haired, heavily built, and scowling, she nodded back.

"Which way to Rainbow Mountain?"

The woman jerked her thumb toward the range of pincushion hills.

"Can you tell us where Zak Stone hangs out?"

"Who wants to know?"

Matt introduced himself and Kirstie and explained their business.

"Sure, I know where he hangs out." The woman's brows practically knitted together with suspicion. "His place is Thunder Lodge. But no way will he see you."

Matt dipped his head to one side. "How come?"

"He don't see no one. He gave up horse doctoring way back."

"Yeah?" Matt was in no hurry to move on, despite a dig in his ribs from Kirstie. "Sorry to hear that."

"Zak had a problem with the state authorities. They said he earned good money giving advice, mixing herbs, healing and all that stuff. Wanted to tax him plenty. Zak said he ain't never earned a cent from working with folks' horses. It was one big mess, I can tell you." The woman was more forthcoming than perhaps she'd intended. She clammed up again now.

"Real sorry." Matt jumped down from the cab and asked for a full tank of fuel. When he climbed back in, he said the woman had given him detailed directions to Thunder Lodge.

"How did you do that?" Kirstie demanded. She was taking deep breaths, wanting to reach their journey's end, yet half-dreading it, staring at the low mountains as if they held a fascinating yet deadly secret.

"Let's say it was my natural charm!" For a few seconds Matt concentrated on getting them back on the road.

The dusty trailer rattled over the rough ground, then settled into the muddy groove worn by other tires. He smiled tensely at Kirstie and flicked on the wipers. "Zak Stone's place is two miles east, then take a left at a haystack, a right where the sign says Thunder Rock, then another left down a narrow culvert. Like the two cowboys and the lovely young lady at the gas station said, 'You can't hardly miss it!'"

8

The road ran out in a dead end. There was a thicket of willows and young aspens, a tall sluice box spilling water into a clear pool. The hills rose steeply to either side, cutting out the view of blue, distant mountains.

"This is the culvert, I guess." Matt climbed down from the cab to take a look around. They'd traveled ten miles on from Bear Claw Creek, following directions yet fearing more and more that the gas station woman had sent them on a wild goose chase. Then they'd spotted the old wooden sign to Thunder Rock and realized they were on the right track after all.

Kirstie followed Matt past the pond, pushing willow branches aside, looking in vain for a cabin or any sign at all that this was the place where Zak Stone lived. "What happened to the road?" she asked.

Matt shrugged. "What happened to electricity?" The overhead cables had run out long before the road, as had any other suggestion of civilization. "And the whole of the twentieth century! Man, I sure wouldn't want to live here!"

They listened to the wind in the aspen trees, went on searching for a track, a fence, a gate—anything that might lead to a house.

"Hear that!" Kirstie held up a warning hand. There was movement up the hillside, beyond the trees. It could be deer or something heavier; maybe elk. Or maybe only her imagination. As she listened again, the woods fell silent.

"C'mon." Matt suggested a retreat to the trailer. "Maybe we can get back to the last cabin on the road and ask more questions." He was already back tracking past the sluice box, stepping carefully around the muddy border of the pond.

But Kirstie stayed behind, gazing into the dripping trees. The aspen leaves were like a green mosaic, shot through with splashes of yellow as the sun broke through the clouds. A white, warm mist covered the rocky ground, and then, as if by magic, the far-off mountain lived up to its name. "Rainbow!" she whispered.

An arc of pure colors rose above the watery landscape, red shading to yellow, green to indigo and violet. It began behind the mountain and ended far off in the west, fading into bruised, blue clouds and more rain.

Kirstie's silence drew the animals from their rocky heights into the stand of aspens, their feet snapping brittle branches, their bodies brushing against wet leaves. Big creatures, their brown, black, and white bodies appearing and disappearing, their snorting breath and heavy, hollow tread familiar to her. There was a glimpse of black-and-white flank, of white mane and a dark, gleaming eye. Then the first horse came into full view.

He was a pinto stallion, strong and proud, his

head big and handsome, his shoulders broad, chest deep. Behind him came a sorrel mare, daintier, with a white blaze running the length of her face. She was leading and protecting a nervous bay foal only two or three months old, his dark mane dripping from the recent rain, his skinny legs covered in mud. None of the horses wore head collars, none were shod. Perhaps they were wild.

Kirstie glanced over her shoulder. She wanted Matt to come back to share the sight of the silent, still creatures who had seen her and come to a wary halt. But he was out of sight past the pond, so she turned back again to study the horses.

Without a sound, a tall, broad man dressed in faded denims had stepped out of the trees between her and the pinto. He blocked her way, looked down at her with a stern, suspicious gaze. His eyes were deep set in a wide, bony face, his long hair tied back, his mouth thin and displeased.

Kirstie gasped and took a step away. She bit back a shout for help, knowing it would make her look dumb and scared. But truly her body was shaking and no words came to her aid as she stared up at the hostile man.

"You lost your way." His deep voice broke the silence. Behind him, the three horses drew nearer.

She shook her head, even though it was a statement, not a question. Kirstie's eyes latched onto a beaded leather sheath at the man's waist containing a glittering blade.

"Yeah, you did. The road goes nowhere."

"We came looking for Zak Stone." She stole another glance at his face, saw no sign of softening, only a blank wall.

"Zak Stone don't want to be found."

Kirstie took a deep breath. This was obviously the man himself: part Native American, a hermit who shunned all visitors. "My horse is sick."

No reply.

"Real sick. He could die." *Please!* she implored with her wide gray eyes. She felt her bottom lip tremble as the man made as if to turn away.

Then he paused. He narrowed his dark brown eyes. "That your horse in the trailer? The palomino?"

"Yes!" He must have been secretly watching them as they drove into the culvert, then taken a look at Lucky as Matt and she explored on foot. This flashed through Kirstie's mind as she seized

120

the only chance she would get to secure Zak Stone's help.

"My brother goes to vet school." She began slowly, then the words poured out. "He couldn't help, so we called in our vet, Glen Woodford. It turns out there was a mix up over Lucky's shots. We had a foal die on us last weekend; he caught an infection from a pony I rescued. We guess my horse got the same bug. Glen's doing tests to find out. Only I didn't wait; I decided to bring Lucky here!" Running out of breath and courage at the same time, Kirstie lowered her gaze.

"You're right—the horse is real sick." Zak Stone let the pinto come and stand beside him, while the sorrel and the foal hung back. The man's face had lost its hard, blank look and turned thoughtful. "The spirit is weak in him."

Kirstie sighed and slumped against the nearest tree, suddenly swamped by a sense of defeat.

"But the light is there," Stone went on. "Faded, like the rainbow when the sun goes, but still within him."

Kirstie shook her head. She was exhausted to the point of admitting defeat. "What does that mean?"

He gazed at her, impassive again. "Your horse's life is in the balance. But he doesn't give in. He fights."

Then she would fight, too. Kirstie hadn't brought Lucky through three states, across mountains and plains to end in doubt and failure.

She drew herself up, met the piercing eye of the legendary horse doctor, spoke out at last. "Save him for me!"

Not a question, a statement. No shadow of doubt. *Trust this man,* a voice said from deep inside, from her heart.

"Wise men of the old nations had a different way of looking at life," Zak Stone told Matt and Kirstie. He'd made himself known to her and agreed to help. Kirstie had run to fetch Matt and now they were unbolting the back of the trailer and letting down the ramp.

"The British and the French came to our wide plains and scorned us, asking why we believed in Wakan Tanka, the Great Mystery. 'Where are the facts to support you in your belief? Where is the science? What is it but old superstition and nonsense?'" Zak spoke matter-of-factly, without resentment. "So the wise men of the tribes answered the ignorant questions with another question: 'What is faith except belief without facts?'"

Matt smiled at Kirstie. "What's logic got to do with it, huh?"

"Yeah, right!" Fumbling at the bolts, she helped lower the ramp and stepped inside the trailer. Lucky gazed at her, almost too weak to lift his head. The veins in his thin face stood out; his eyes were dull. "What did I tell you?" she said, going right up to him and cradling his head in the crook of her arm. "This is Rainbow Mountain. Didn't I say I knew there was someone special here who could help?"

"Bring him out, Kirstie." Matt sounded anxious. "I've got a blanket out here to keep him warm. The sooner we get moving the more chance we have."

"No. No blanket, and take your time," Zak advised. He looked like he never hurried or raised his voice.

"Anyway, I have no choice." She noticed that the stiffness in Lucky's legs was worse, that the fetlock joints visible above the trailer bandages had swollen to twice their normal size. Given his weak condition, she knew that moving fast was beyond him.

So she soothed and tempted him down the ramp, talking all the while, but shocked when she brought him into the daylight to see how lifeless his golden coat had turned, how thin he'd grown over the last four or five days. His tense jaw and arched back showed what a strain it was to make even the small amount of effort involved in walking out of the trailer.

"There's open grazing land behind the sluice box," Zak told her, leading the way past the running water, down a grassy track between willow bushes. He'd taken in Lucky's weakened state and said it was important for him to drink and rest for the remainder of the day.

"What else?" Kirstie asked, as step by step she encouraged Lucky along the track. Ahead she saw a green meadow surrounded by trees and rocks, a natural enclosure where her horse would be safe. But she expected more action from Zak. "When do we start to heal him?"

"We already started," Zak replied. "We give him

time to drink spring water, for the sun to shine on him, for the moon to rise and look down."

"Yeah, but..." She wondered about herbs and old native medicines, but Zak's stern look had returned so she fell silent. Instead of bothering him with questions, she simply led Lucky into the middle of the meadow, released him from his head collar and stepped back.

The horse doctor nodded. "The spirit of Thunder Rock will find him here," he explained. "He'll protect your horse from harm. Tomorrow, when Lucky is stronger, we'll take him to the rock and talk to the spirit."

"You want me to leave him here?" Kirstie understood, but she hesitated. Lucky was sick and confused; surely he needed her to stay close.

Zak looked at the panic in her eyes. "Trust the spirit," he told her.

Boy, this was hard! Lucky was so weak he could hardly stand. Every breath looked like it might be his last. Yet Zak Stone was saying walk away—leave him in this strange green prison. And she had to do it. If this was going to work, she must follow exactly what the guy said.

"Kirstie?" Matt murmured. He stood on the track with Zak.

"Don't worry, I'll be close by," she whispered to Lucky. "Call if you need me."

Thunder Lodge, where Zak Stone had lived for more than thirty years, was a small, two-roomed cabin at the foot of a sheer, overhanging cliff. A stream ran by its door, feeding a small wooden water tower powered by a steam pump. There was a high woodpile in the porch and a small corral where the backwoods man would keep his pinto, his sorrel, and her foal during the long winter months.

Inside, all was kept neat and clean. A plain table stood in the center of the main room on a floor covered by a red and black patterned rug. There was a sink with one tap, a wood-burning stove, a window without drapes overlooking the stream. The room, smelling of pine and woodsmoke, had no ornaments, no personal possessions except those few pots and pans which Zak used for cooking.

He stood in the doorway with Matt and Kirstie, looking out at the setting sun. Lennie Goodman's trailer, the only reminder of modern life, was parked by the sluice box out of sight.

"So why did you break your rule and decide to help us?" Matt asked, going to sit on the porch step, his long legs stretched out, his boot tapping a rhythm on the grass. "The woman in Bear Claw Creek said no way would you do any more work with sick horses."

"Blame your sister." Zak's gaze didn't flicker from the far horizon. "The girl would just about give up her life for that horse. Who am I to turn her away?"

"So why stop the good work in the first place?" Curiosity drove Matt on. "If you have a gift, why not use it?"

Zak shrugged. "Folks bothered me," was all he said. Then he got to talking about the past. He said he did remember a guy from a ranch in Colorado and a pinto horse called Bandit. "Smart horse," he murmured, nothing more.

But when Matt asked him to go further back in time to tell them about his roots, he opened up willingly. He was part Sioux Indian, he confirmed. "My great-grandfather was a Teton, a buffalo hunter. His grandfather was brother to Red Cloud. He fought at Little Bighorn with Sitting Bull."

The names from the past impressed Kirstie and made her sad. She thought of warriors in buckskin with buffalo-horn headdresses, of treaties made and broken, of lands taken away. And she could picture Zak Stone as part of that tradition, as he gazed at the sunset with his proud head held high.

"My own grandfather was born on a reservation in Montana. He married a French Canadian woman and went fur trapping in the North." He described in his own family history the break-up of a way of life. "When he died in a hunting accident, his wife and children moved to Montreal. My mother was brought up in the city, the youngest of seven children. I never knew my father. He and my mother didn't marry, and he left her before I was born."

"So what brought you back from Canada?" Kirstie asked quietly. There was nothing to disturb the conversation except the stream running over rocks and jays calling from tall pine trees on the overhanging cliff.

"There was nothing for me in Montreal. I was a kid, just drifting, picking up scraps about the past the way you do. So I drifted south, wound up in Bear Claw Creek with a beat-up motorbike and a head full of stuff about my ancestors." Zak grinned at this distant memory of himself. "This was thirty-five years ago. I'd been over to the reservation in Montana where my grandpa was born, learned all the stuff about healing. Let's just say I found out it was my thing."

"So you came out here, built your cabin and stayed for thirty-five years." Matt stood up and stretched.

"I guess I like it," came the understated reply.

Stealing a glance at Zak, Kirstie saw that he was smiling. The first time that had happened since they met, she realized. It changed her view of him totally to see the even white teeth, the creases in the skin around his eyes. "You like it until guys like us come poking around bothering you!" she countered.

"Yeah, well." The smile faded on a shrug. "Wait here," he told her, disappearing inside the cabin and coming back out with a hammock made of skins and leather thongs. He thrust it into her hands without explanation.

"What's this for?"

"You wanna sleep out in the meadow?"

"With Lucky?" She nodded eagerly. "Yeah, but—"

"I said you wouldn't help the horse get better by sticking around?" he interrupted. "Sure, I know."

"So why this?" She untangled the leather strips and found out how the thing worked.

"It's not to help the horse get through the night. It's so you don't lie awake in the cabin fretting yourself sick."

"Right." She glanced excitedly at Matt, who nodded. "I get to sleep under the stars with Lucky!"

Kirstie swung in the hammock, staring up at the moon. She thought of her mom running Half Moon Ranch without her and Matt, of Lisa and the friendship bracelets they exchanged each year. Slipping her fingers through the one she wore on her wrist, she sighed.

Nearby Lucky stirred. He took a step or two toward her, his dark shape outlined by moonlight, his mane and tail showing up white in the shadows. Stiff, poor guy, and still fighting for breath, his lungs possibly damaged beyond repair. Standing in the shadows, he gave off the confused aimlessness of all animals who are sick.

Kirstie turned her head and caught the gleam of his eye. "You listen to me," she murmured. "There's a spirit out here taking care of you, OK? It lives in the mountain, or maybe in the air; I don't know exactly. Something to do with Wakan Tanka."

Lucky gazed patiently at her swinging gently in her hammock. In...out, in...out—his breath rattled.

"This spirit is a great power and for some reason it likes Zak. The way I see things, it's given him a special gift. If Zak goes up the mountain and talks

to it, he can call up the spirit and use it to heal horses who are sick."

Silence on Rainbow Mountain. Deep, dark night.

"OK, boy?" Kirstie whispered, her voice shaking. "Yeah, I know, this stuff gets weirder. And you want to know the weirdest thing of all about the Great Mystery?" She swung out of her hammock and went to stroke a trembling Lucky. "I really, really believe it's gonna work!"

9

In the gray dawn light Zak Stone came to get Kirstie and Lucky.

"This is the good time," he said, a faraway look in his dark eyes.

Kirstie struggled out of a deep sleep. She'd dreamed of herds of wild horses galloping over golden plains, their limbs fluid, coats gleaming. The dream horses made no noise, their hooves seeming not to touch the ground as they swept across the valley toward mountains lost in purple haze.

Now she opened her eyes to cold dew and white mist on the ground. Quickly she unzipped her sleeping bag and tipped herself out of the hammock. She saw Lucky standing patiently nearby, his coat wet, his broken stance suggesting the continued agony of hardly being able to breathe. And she could hear the gasping intake of air, the long, slow rattle out again, which told her that he was, as yet, no better.

"Where's Matt?" she mumbled, zipping up the fleece jacket that she'd kept on all night. Her tangled hair tumbled over her face; she shivered as she gazed around the enclosed green meadow.

"Still sleeping." Zak offered no explanation, but made it clear that Matt's presence on the mountain wasn't needed. Taking deep breaths, he began to concentrate on Lucky, walking in a slow circle around him, taking in every symptom of his sickness: the horse's drooping head and swollen limbs, the strange, double heave of his ribs as he breathed out. Coming full circle to where Kirstie waited, he nodded then walked on.

This must mean it was time to talk to the spirits. For a second or two, Kirstie panicked. Would she need a head collar and lead rope? Should she be there at all? Or was it just down to Zak Stone and Lucky?

The answer to the first question was no. As if he understood something of what was happening, Lucky followed the tall, silent man out of the meadow. Each step was painful and difficult—down the grassy track, past the sluice box where water spouted and tumbled into the pool, up a stony slope toward the cliff top which overhung Zak's cabin.

Still in doubt, Kirstie watched Lucky's slow progress. Only when Zak reached the top of the cliff, turned and gestured for her to come, did she set off after them. She scrambled quickly up the slope, sending loose stones rattling downhill, disturbing a ground squirrel who'd been peering out of long grass. The squirrel in turn set off a couple of jays who screeched and clattered out of the branch of a pine tree then swooped and landed on the roof of Zak's cabin below.

Reaching the flat, wide ledge, she rested one hand on Lucky's shoulder, trying to make out some special feature that would set the place apart. To the right was the sheer drop of about fifty feet, to the left a series of smooth, strangely shaped boulders, marked with crevices where lichens and blue, bell-shaped flowers grew. "Is this Thunder Rock?" she asked.

For answer, Zak continued along the ledge. He disappeared into the mist behind the tallest of the boulders.

Kirstie ran after him, down a narrow channel between two high rocks. "How far is it? I don't think Lucky can make it much further!"

Zak's face, only just visible in the dark, damp shadows, was impassive. He stood waiting for the horse, who stumbled along after them. His hooves echoed down the hollow tunnel, his breath was halting, his progress agonizingly slow.

Then the rocks opened out onto a second, domed ledge from where Kirstie could see for miles. Hills rolled away from them in the silent dawn, rising to snowcapped peaks in the far distance. The ledge faced east, and as she, Zak, and Lucky emerged, she saw a sliver of red sun appear from behind a mountain, lighting up the gray sky. The Big Sky. Kirstie looked up as the glow from the sun spread, turning everything it touched from sleep to waking, from cold to life-giving warmth.

"This is Thunder Rock," Zak said, pointing to a huge expanse of dark gray granite, still in the shadows. It rose like a whale's back to their right, bare and stern, some thirty feet above the ledge. "The home of the spirits."

Kirstie nodded and narrowed her eyes, standing close to Lucky and putting a protective arm around his neck.

As they turned away from the rock to face the rising sun, light spilled across the valley. It touched Kirstie's face with a promise of warmth, slid across the ledge, and tipped the rounded peak of Thunder Rock. Gray granite glittered pink.

"Bring your horse to the foot of the rock and stay there with him," Zak told her. "Understand that the great horse spirit dwells here in Thunder Rock and that I will ask him to protect Lucky and take away his sickness."

Shaking, Kirstie obeyed. She led her beloved palomino into the cold shadow at the foot of Thunder Rock, fearing, hoping...

Quietly Zak began. "I call upon the Great Spirit,

the all powerful god, Wakan Tanka. I ask him to send his spirit to this rock to protect and heal this horse."

In the long silence, facing the east, Kirstie kept her hand on Lucky's quivering neck. She saw the sun melt the shadows and raise the mist, shining bright across the valley.

Facing them, his face dark yet serene, Zak breathed slow and deep. He raised his hands skyward, gazing intently, eyes following a shape which seemed to swoop down from the sky and settle above Lucky's head. When Kirstie turned to glance over her shoulder, expecting perhaps an eagle or a hawk, she saw nothing.

"Mighty spirit, I accept your presence in the great dawning of a new day," Zak whispered. He lowered his hands and bowed his head.

Kirstie felt a pressure on her chest. She had to gasp for breath, closed her eyes to steady herself before she breathed out slowly. Opening them, she found Zak at Lucky's side.

"In this moment, in this dwelling place of the spirits, come to me, Wakan Tanka. Work your Great Mystery through these hands."

He reached out and placed his broad palms on Lucky's trembling back, kept them there until he felt the horse's muscles relax. Then he moved his hands slowly over the feeble, ailing body, passing them over his ribcage, bringing them up to his head. Through it all, the horse stood perfectly still, ears pricked as if listening to something beyond the silence, as if watching a sign in the deepening blue of the sky.

Breathe! Kirstie reminded herself. She drew air into her lungs. *Breathe!* she told Lucky. *Deep and easy.*

Zak cupped his hands over Lucky's nostrils and leaned his head against the horse's head. He held the position in intense, silent concentration.

There was a breeze from the valley. It lifted Lucky's white mane and ran a shiver down the length of his golden back.

"Breathe!" Kirstie whispered.

Slowly Lucky raised his head and drew a deep, steady breath of cool air.

Zak stepped back, his work complete.

"So, no drums, no dancing?" Matt asked abruptly.

Perched in the fork of an aspen tree, legs swinging, her back against the silver-white trunk, Kirstie shook her head. "No. And I didn't see a single feather or bead necklace, no fringed deerskin pants, nothing!" As far as traditional dress and music went, the healing ceremony at Thunder Rock could be said to have fallen far short of expectations.

"So tell me!" Matt demanded to know what had gone on. He'd woken in an empty cabin, with the sun streaming in through the window. By the time he'd dressed and made it to the meadow, Kirstie

140

and Lucky were already back from the rock, and Zak was nowhere to be seen.

"It was amazing!" Kirstie sighed. She kept her eyes glued on Lucky, who was quietly grazing at the far side of the culvert.

"That doesn't tell me anything! What happened exactly?" It was obvious from the frown creasing his forehead that Matt wished he'd been there to witness the healing ceremony. Leaving him behind had made him irritable.

"I can't describe it." How did you say that an invisible spirit had moved in the breeze and breathed new life into a sick horse?

"Try. Did he use herbs?"

"Nope."

"Magic spells?"

"Nope."

Matt strode around the tree, exasperated and skeptical. "What then?"

Kirstie jumped down to the ground and made her way toward Lucky. "Just faith, I guess."

"Huh? And did it work?" He followed across the grass, striding ahead to confront her.

But she refused to answer. Sidestepping him,

she stood, arms crossed, studying Lucky. He was still weak, no way his normal self. His coat didn't shine the way it should; he moved awkwardly on those swollen joints. But he was eating contentedly, head down, cropping at the grass and chewing hard. "Listen!" she told Matt.

They heard water trickling through the meadow, leaves rustling.

"What am I supposed to hear?" he demanded.

"Is Lucky struggling for breath?" Kirstie asked, her eyes sparkling, still listening hard as if she couldn't believe the evidence of her own ears.

Matt stared at the smooth motion of Lucky's ribcage, in and out without the shuddering double-heave of aborted breath. He shook his head.

"So it worked!"

Thanks to Zak Stone, whatever he did and however he did it, Lucky could breathe easy.

"A horse can sometimes battle against a virus and pull through," Matt the college-trained skeptic pointed out. "Equine influenza is serious but isn't fatal in 100 percent of cases, especially if the horse is young and healthy."

It was Friday evening: twelve hours since Thunder Rock. Zak had stayed away all day, leaving the cabin to Matt and Kirstie, apparently confident that Lucky's healing had taken effect. The sun had traveled across a blue sky unbroken by clouds, blazing down from its midday height and only now cooling as the shadows lengthened and it sank in the west. Lucky had fed and drunk without a break, making up for the starving, fever-ridden days just past.

At dusk Kirstie had fetched a grooming kit from the trailer, and started work on cleaning Lucky up. She'd brushed the dust out of his coat, raising clouds of the stuff after a week of neglect. She'd been picking dirt out of his hooves when Matt had come along and started into his "There's gotta be a logical explanation" routine.

"The trachea and lungs can recover once the body's natural healing mechanisms kick in to defeat the infection," he explained, cool and reasonable. "Fever constricts the blood vessels, leading to lack of oxygen in the lungs, but, as long as the horse rests, the damage is reversed as soon as his temperature's back to normal."

143

"Sure, Matt." Kirstie hooked a stone out of a back hoof, her hair swinging forward across her face. "And that happens in a second, like this?" She snapped her fingers and shot him a frowning glance.

He hesitated then came back. "It could happen!"

"And why does it have to be scientific?" she demanded, hooking out more packed dirt. "Why can't it be a spiritual thing?"

Struggling for an answer, frowning and about to resort to more college stuff, he suddenly changed his mind. "Because I wasn't there," he confessed quietly and honestly. "What I didn't see is real hard for me to believe."

"And I was, and I do," she replied. "We were, weren't we, Lucky? We believe."

Zak came back at nightfall on his big black-and-white pinto. He rode bareback, with a head collar and rope, no bit or bridle. There was no mention of Thunder Rock.

Supper was bacon, eggs, and hash browns, cooked on his wood stove. The two men drank homemade beer, talked about baseball and cars, discussed the best route for Kirstie, Matt, and Lucky to take through Wyoming, missing the busy tourist roads of Yellowstone Park.

At ten, when Kirstie slipped away with a handful of oats for Lucky, she found that Zak had followed her to the meadow.

"How is he?" he asked, looming up in the darkness, his footsteps making no noise.

"Good!" She felt Lucky's soft mouth take the food from her hand. Then his rough tongue licked between her fingers. "He's eating plenty and the swellings are down."

"Hmm." Zak's nod was brief but satisfied. "Your brother, Matt..." he began.

"Take no notice!" Kirstie jumped in. "He doesn't mean anything." She wanted to say sorry. Though Matt hadn't exactly behaved badly over supper, he'd sure been acting as if Thunder Rock had never happened.

"It's cool," Zak shrugged and spoke without regret. "Your brother is a twenty-first-century man. He has different gods. I belong in the nineteenth century, or before. That's why I live out here, minding my business. I'm a kind of throwback, a mistake."

She nodded that she understood. It sounded a lonely life, yet somehow she knew that for Zak it wasn't. "Today was special," she confided quietly, one hand gently stroking Lucky's face. She answered Zak's widening smile with one of her own, there in the heart of the tiny piece of paradise where he'd built his life. "This morning you did something for the two of us that we'll never ever forget!"

10

"Hey, Kirstie," Matt muttered.

"Yeah?" She was half asleep in the passenger seat, a day and a half into the journey home to Half Moon Ranch. A white road ran between ripening corn as far as the eye could see. In the back of the trailer, Lucky was tucking into his hay, resting and building up his strength.

"About Zak..." he began, then hesitated.

Kirstie glanced sideways at her brother's profile: dark hair falling forward over a flat forehead, straight nose, square chin. He was so like their dad in the photographs in the family album, taken when Dad had been a college student, too. "Yeah, what about Zak?"

"I've been thinking—maybe I was a little tough on him."

"Did you give him a hard time? What did you say?" Kirstie took her feet down from the dashboard and swiveled around.

"Nothing." Matt shrugged, then frowned. "Exactly that. Nothing, zilch! Like if I'm dealing with a person's sick horse, the least I expect is a word of thanks, a handshake."

"Too late now." Kirstie thought of the hundreds of miles between them and Rainbow Mountain. "I guess this is why Zak likes to be alone up there. Maybe he grew tired of trying to explain the way he did things to guys like you!" For a few moments, Kirstie enjoyed making Matt feel guilty. Then she decided to let him off the hook. "Hey, he understood where you were coming from, OK."

Matt glanced at her. "He did?"

"Yeah. He called you a twenty-first-century man."

Kirstie remembered her own good-bye to Zak

Stone in the small corral at Thunder Lodge. He'd been working with the little bay foal, doing join-up work while the sorrel mare looked on. When he'd realized that Kirstie, Lucky, and Matt were loaded up and ready to go, he'd come slowly to the fence.

"Look after that palomino when you get him home," he'd told her, the rare smile creasing his broad features. "He's a horse worth taking care of."

She'd nodded, unable to reply.

"May the Spirit go with you," Zak had murmured, turning back to his horses.

Broad shoulders in a denim jacket, gentle hands caressing the sorrel mare—that had been Kirstie's last view of Zak Stone.

"... Hey, Matt," she said now. They were clear of the fields of corn, heading into mountains, thinking of home.

"Yeah?"

"Thanks."

"For what?"

She smiled and looked ahead to Longs Peak. "Just thanks, that's all!"

* * *

Lucky got two weeks of rest in Red Fox Meadow, and the best care Kirstie could give. Each day he put on weight; each day his coat when she brushed it grew softer, healthier, more shiny.

"Come up to the ranch for the Midsummer Barbecue," Kirstie said to Lisa over the phone. "Afterward we can ride out on Five Mile Creek Trail."

It would be the first time she'd put a saddle on Lucky since he'd fallen sick. She would take things easy, be sure not to ask too much of him by riding up the steeper trails. Riverside would be best.

"Nervous?" Sandy asked, coming away from a bunch of guests gathered around the barbecue when she saw the girls taking saddles and bridles out to the meadow.

Kirstie nodded, glad when her mom walked along with them. The sun had sunk low in the sky, but the summer air was still warm, the blue irises and other marsh flowers growing by the creek giving off a heavy scent.

"Well, Lucky sure looks fine to me," Lisa said as they came to the fence. The palomino was easy to pick out from the herd with his glossy golden coat and blond mane. When he saw Kirstie, he lifted his head and came trotting smartly toward her.

"Hey, Kirstie, hey, Lisa!" Charlie called as he led Johnny Mohawk and Yukon into the meadow after a day's work riding the trails. "Kirstie, you taking Lucky out?"

"Sure!" she called back. "First time!"

"Good luck!" the young wrangler said as he unfastened the two lead ropes and sent the black gelding and the brown and white paint on their way. "I'll tell Matt and Hadley," he promised, heading back to the corral.

"Hey, no!" Kirstie didn't want any more onlookers. "Jeez!" she sighed when Charlie ignored her.

"Go ahead, saddle your horse," Sandy told her. "I want to see you ride out of here into the sunset, like in the movies." She turned with a quiet smile to help Lisa with Snowflake. "It's gonna be fine," she told them as she tightened the cinch strap and checked the bit. "No problem."

"You hear?" Fastening Lucky's cheek strap, Kirstie had a quiet word in his ear.

The horse twitched under the weight of the saddle and stamped his feet, eager to be off.

"This is your big day," she whispered, noticing Charlie strolling back with Matt and Hadley plus a small group of guests. She double checked his cinch, ran her hands across the firm muscles of his shoulder and neck. "You look great, OK?"

He flicked his ears then dipped his head.

"The vet signed you off, you know that? When we got you back in one piece from Rainbow Mountain, Glen said it was a miracle, remember? That's you, Lucky, a miracle of old-fashioned science!"

Up went the head with a tug of the reins. *C'mon, let's go!*

Lisa was already up in the saddle, chatting with Matt and Charlie. She laughed while she waited, her white T-shirt standing out in the lengthening shadows. "You first!" she called to Kirstie as Hadley held the gate open.

One foot in the broad stirrup, the other leg swinging across Lucky's broad back, settling into the saddle with a creak of leather...A deep breath.

Hadley nodded up at her as she rode Lucky forward. "Good job!" he murmured.

Praise from Hadley. Wow!

Then they were out of Red Fox Meadow, heading

for the creek, Lisa and Snowflake following
hind. Lucky's footing was sound on the fir
his gait even as he broke into a trot along
So far so good.

"See, he's going great!" Lisa caught
low sun caught her face and lit up her t
red curls.

Strong and even as Kirstie sat the trot
ran alongside the clear, fast-running cree
felt the wind tug at her hair, sensed her
confidence grow. He swerved sideways to
a clump of willows, dipped his feet in the
splashed clear again.

"Yeah!" Lisa called, making Snowflake pi
speed, taking a higher track away from the w
edge. She urged her horse from a trot to a
He lengthened his stride and took off tow
Hummingbird Rock.

For a second Kirstie held Lucky back.
glanced over her shoulder at the knot of onlook
watching from the white fence, still able to pick
the slight, blonde figure of her mom. Sandy wav
both arms above her head. The others yelled.

"Yee-hah! Go, Kirstie!"

So she went. She sat deep in the saddle and gave Lucky his head. He dipped back onto his haunches and launched himself from the bank into the creek, thundering knee-deep along the riverbed, churning up spray.

"Go, Lucky!" Kirstie whispered.

His hooves smacked the water, kicked it up shoulder high, and soaked her to the skin. She crouched low over his back, laughing at the speed, yelling out at the cold, tingling spray as it drove into her face.

Lucky raced on in an ecstasy of freedom and power. This was what he remembered: he and Kirstie galloping through meadows, along river banks, plowing through water.

He stretched out his head and pounded on. The spray he raised was caught in the last rays of the sun. A million drops, a rainbow of multicolored light.